Horace Broussard knows he needs to learn how to say no to his brother, Herbert. His older, larger brother always seems to drag him into trouble. Except, the two times he'd gathered the courage, Herbert had explained why it was a bad idea . . . with his fists and feet. The first time had left him pissing blood for days. The second time had culminated in a broken wrist. Horace doesn't say no to his brother anymore, which is how he ends up poaching gators in the swamp . . . again.

When they spot a small pack of wolves running through the cypress trees, Herbert orders that they go after them, claiming a wolf pelt on his floor would be cool.

Just like many of Herbert's bad ideas, Horace ends up in hot water. They're caught by the owners of the wolves—a fierce biker gang. Except, then something crazy happens. A huge African elephant grabs Horace in its trunk and carries him into the swamp. When other animals arrive and turn into men, he wonders if he's hit his head and is hallucinating. Can the paranormal be real, and if so, how can he keep this revelation from his dominating brother?

Reader Advisory: The first chapter of this tale overlaps with the last chapter in Pursuit by Camelback.

The Swamp Elephant
Copyright © 2022 Charlie Richards
ISBN: 978-1-4874-3793-0
Cover art by Angela Waters

Published by eXtasy Books Inc

Look for us online at:
www.eXtasybooks.com

THE SWAMP ELEPHANT
KONTRA'S MENAGERIE 34

BY

CHARLIE RICHARDS

CHAPTER ONE

Taking a sip of coffee, Horace Broussard hid his wince. He didn't care for coffee at the best of times, but his brother's coffee tasted even more vile. Herbert loved strong coffee. He claimed it put hair on his chest.

Horace didn't think Herbert needed more hair on his chest. His older brother had plenty of body hair, and he liked to lounge in his boxer briefs most evenings watching TV, which showed it off. It was *not* a good look, so Horace spent most evenings out back whittling, enjoying the fresh night air.

When Horace scooped two heaping spoonfuls of sugar into his coffee, he ignored Herbert's sneer.

Whatever.

It was better than trying to choke down Herbert's vile excuse that he called coffee. Normally, Horace made the coffee in the mornings. He was usually up at least an hour before his brother because the man expected breakfast to be ready for him first thing.

So why the crapballs is Herbert up at seven AM on a Saturday?

Horace knew for a fact that Herbert hadn't gotten in from the bar until nearly midnight. His brother had made a hell of a lot of noise coming in — so had his fuck for the evening. The woman's giggles and moans had given Horace the creeps.

God, how can guys think those sorts of noises are sexy?

Having known he was gay since the age of fourteen, Horace had been damn careful to keep it under wraps. Ten years later, he was still a virgin, and he figured he would remain that way until the day he died . . . or Herbert died.

1

Unless I figure out a way to get away from my brother.

Unfortunately, Horace's couple of prior attempts hadn't gone so well.

Horace shut down those thoughts, not wanting to think about the injuries he'd ended up with. Instead, he pulled out a couple of skillets and started breakfast.

"Hurry up," Herbert ordered, sitting at the table with his coffee. "I wanna get out on the water."

"The water?" Even as Horace couldn't help but ask, he grabbed the bacon and eggs from the fridge.

"Yup. Got a tip last night from Florent." Herbert's grin didn't soothe Horace's unease upon finding his brother already awake and waiting for him in the kitchen. His next words only made his gut twist even more. "He spotted a clutch of gator eggs near Great Cypress Swamp." After slurping his coffee, Herbert claimed, "It'll be quiet out there this time of the morning. Let's go get us some gators."

As Horace flipped the three over-easy eggs for Herbert, he couldn't help but comment, "Gators aren't in season."

In fact, they wouldn't be for months.

With a snort, Herbert sneered. "I don't give a shit."

Of course, he didn't.

Horace grimaced as he flipped the bacon in a second skillet. "I'll, uh, I'll get the boat gassed up for you while you eat," he offered, hoping to avoid his brother dragging him along with him.

"Naw, I'll do it while you clean the kitchen and eat," Herbert told him. "Hurry up with the food. We need to get a move on."

Swallowing his unhappy sigh, Horace obeyed his brother and quickly finished making his brother's breakfast. He set a plate with the over-easy eggs as well as two slices of toast, heavily buttered, and half a dozen strips of bacon. Then he returned to the stove and cracked two more eggs into the pan. After scrambling them, he began crunching his way through his first of the four bacon strips he'd kept for himself. Then Horace began cleaning up the toaster crumbs and bacon pan while waiting for his eggs.

Once the eggs were done, Horace loaded them onto his two slices of toast. He picked up the first one and started eating. Out of the corner of his eye, he noticed that Herbert had finished his food. Horace moved toward the table as he polished off his toast and eggs.

Herbert drained his coffee before leaving the mug on the table beside the plate. Rising, he told him, "I'll get the boat ready. Don't be long."

As Herbert left the room, Horace picked up his brother's dishes. Once the man had left out the back door, he allowed himself to shake his head. He sighed deeply. After placing the dishes in the sink, Horace turned on the water before rubbing his palms over his face.

"I wonder if he'd track me down if I went to New Orleans," Horace muttered under his breath. "Maybe I could lose myself in the big city long enough for him to decide to leave me alone."

Except, as Horace cleaned the kitchen, he didn't think that was possible. His brother had his buddies keeping an eye on him not only when he was at work but also when he did something as mundane as grocery shopping. His brother didn't plan to let his servant go anywhere.

After Horace had finished eating and cleaning the kitchen, he hurried to his bedroom. He quickly changed into an old shirt and a faded pair of jeans with fray-holes starting to form along the seams. Horace pulled an old flannel shirt over his tee before tugging on a pair of socks.

Horace padded through the small house to the back door. Stepping on the back porch, he spotted his brother sitting in the boat, doing something with the engine. As Horace tugged on his hiking boots, he could say one thing for the man, Herbert was good with engines. Otherwise, the small boat would have crapped out years ago.

"This is going to suck," Horace muttered as he trudged down to the dock.

As Horace climbed into the boat, Herbert fired up the engine. He'd just settled onto the bench seat, propping his feet against the side to keep himself steady, when his brother hit the throttle. Gripping the side of the boat, Horace watched their dock and home quickly disappear between the cypress trees.

Nearly three hours later, Horace helped Herbert wrangle their third gator to the side of the boat. He turned his attention to the right as he watched his brother prepare to shoot the gator in the head. At least that would be a kill shot, and the beast wouldn't suffer.

"Holy shit," Horace whispered, blinking in shock. "No freakin' way."

Surely he wasn't seeing what he thought he was seeing. His focus slipped as he took in the animals loping on the bank, and his grip on the rope holding the gator loosened.

"What?" Herbert grunted. "Keep the damn line taut."

"There are wolves in the bayou," Horace whispered, struggling to yank his attention away from the three beasts jumping agilely from dirt to cypress roots and back to dirt again.

"There are what?" Herbert straightened and focused on where Horace was looking. "Well, fuck." The man's mean chuckle filled the air. "One of those heads would look great on my wall and the skin on my floor." Herbert shifted in his seat, waving a hand and adding, "Let the line go. We'll come back for it."

Herbert leveled his revolver at the trio of wolves.

"Wait!" Horace cried, realizing he should have kept his

mouth shut. *God, when will I learn?* "What are you doing?"

"Hunting wolves," Herbert stated with a clear *duh* in his voice. "Stop moving!"

Horace hadn't even realized he'd been shifting on his seat toward Herbert. What he planned to do, he had no idea. He just really didn't want to see his brother kill a wolf. Although, why they would be in the swamp, he had no idea.

Upon hearing Herbert's snarled order, Horace instinctively froze. A second later, he heard his brother take the shot. His ears began to ring even as he jerked his focus back to the wolves.

The trio had frozen — two black wolves and one gray one — and were staring in their direction. As Herbert took another shot, they spun in uniform and disappeared between the trees. Horace let out a silent sigh of relief.

It seems my brother missed.

Horace couldn't say he was surprised, considering Herbert didn't practice much. Normally, he was shooting a gator at point-blank range. That meant he wasn't much at aiming.

"Damn it," Herbert growled, shoving his revolver into the holster at his hip. "Hang on."

Then Herbert fired up their boat's engine and gunned it.

Horace grabbed wildly for the side of the boat, nearly being flung over the side as Herbert spun them around. Then he went tearing up the bayou. Planting his feet on the other side, Horace clung tightly as his brother zig-zagged through the swamp, barely missing cypress roots, branches, and other debris in his pursuit of the wolves.

Horace could see them ahead, but they were gaining.

Herbert leaned forward, pulled out his gun, and aimed again.

The bang of the firearm was making his ears ring, and Horace desperately wanted to rub his ears but refused to let go for fear of falling overboard.

"Watch out!" Horace cried, spotting the partially submerged wood up ahead.

Herbert wrenched the throttle stick, turning them sharply. The boat lurched and rocked, bouncing awkwardly off the side of the stump. Careening to the left, the boat's bow slammed into the muddy bank, driving them halfway up it.

"Damn it," Herbert snarled. Leaning forward, he smacked Horace upside the back of his head. "You fucker. You distracted me."

Horace hunched his shoulders, leaning away from Herbert's next hit. He knew it wouldn't do any good to point out that he'd saved them from a head-on collision. His damn brother had been too busy trying to poach wolves.

Asshole.

"Put the gun down, asshole," a deep voice ordered.

Gaping, Horace stared up at the scariest-looking guy he'd seen in . . . well, ever. He had a huge, thickly muscled build and had to stand six-foot-six, although it was tough to tell, considering he stood up on the bank. The guy's brawny, tattooed arms were crossed over his expansive chest, and his goateed lips were curved into a fierce scowl. Even the flecks of silvery-gray threading through his hair didn't soften his appearance. In fact, somehow, Horace thought it made him look even more menacing.

Or maybe that's the cold anger in his deep brown eyes.

Adding to the intimidation factor, there were two more beefy bruisers flanking scary guy number one.

Oh, we are so fucked.

Herbert—of course, the moron that he was—tried to turn his gun on the guys.

The pale-featured brown-haired man with a scar bisecting his left brow and curving down his cheek, lunged forward. A second later, he was gripping Herbert's wrist. He must have used a pressure point or something, because a second later, Herbert howled in pain and dropped the gun . . . right into the waters of the swamp.

Oh, damn. He's going to be pissed about losing that later. I bet he's going to make me search for it, too.

"Get out of the boat." The second guy who was flanking scary-guy one held out his hand, palm up. The man's ebony skin glistened with sweat in the Louisiana heat. There was a serious gleam to his black eyes, but his expression appeared encouraging as opposed to angry like the other two. "Come on, young one. You have nowhere to go."

Well, I'll have to look for it if I make it out of this alive.

Doing as the black man with the slightly accented voice ordered, Horace took the guy's hand. The man helped him from the boat, his movements gentle, as opposed to the pair who were all but bodily lifting a cussing Herbert. His brother bucked his body, trying to wrench away from them, but they easily subdued him and began frog-marching him through the swamp.

The black man placed a hand on Horace's shoulder — light but firm — and guided him after the trio. After hiking only about a hundred yards, a clearing appeared, revealing an older Victorian home in obvious stages of repair. Men milled around the area, doing different tasks from painting to sanding to fixing boards on the deck.

One thing they all seemed to have in common, however, was the fact that they all paused to glare at Horace and his brother.

Shit.

There were over a dozen motorcycles lined up in the detached garage, easily seen through the open door.

The wolves were sitting at the base of the steps, two of them growling softly. They didn't advance on them, however. Instead, they sat, obviously obeying the big goateed guy.

Oh, we are so fucked. Herbert shot at a hidden biker gangs' wolves!

As Horace had gotten lost in his spiraling thoughts, his

mind threatening to shut down in shock and fear, another man had joined their captors. He had his hand on Herbert's head, and he was staring into his brother's eyes. His odd, lavender gaze seemed to have entranced Herbert, for he now stood quietly.

When the pale bald man turned that lavender gaze on Horace, a shudder worked through him. The guy reached for him, and he nearly pissed himself. He tried to rear back, but his body was frozen, not obeying his commands.

At first, Horace thought the trembles working through him were his body's reaction to the bikers. Except, the vibrations intensified, and he heard a bugling noise he didn't recognize. To his confusion, the men paused and looked left.

Horace followed their actions, and his blood rushed to his head as a fresh wave of shock filled him. The bugling noise had come from an elephant—*a fucking elephant!*

With the sound of the blood rushing through his ears, Horace couldn't follow the conversation. All he could think about was the fact that the elephant was wrapping his trunk around his body. He was being lifted into the air. Then he was tucked against the huge animal's chest and being carried away from the bikers.

I'm being kidnapped by an elephant.

The crazy thought entered his mind, then was gone . . . because it was lights out.

CHAPTER TWO

The scent of the human that Alpha Kontra and his men had brought into the clearing had nearly blown Donovan's mind. He knew he was supposed to stay hidden when strangers were around—since he couldn't shift into his human form, yet—but he just couldn't. Getting close to the human drove every other thought out of Donovan's mind.

My mate! The human is my mate!

I finally understand why Rudy nearly charged into the clearing, even with the feds here.

Donovan had wrapped his trunk around the camel shifter's leg, stopping his actions. Still, after Donovan had let go, Rudy had waited. Once the feds had left, he and Mutegi—a warthog shifter and Alpha Kontra's head enforcer—had figured out that Rudy had scented his mate, who'd ended up being the human the feds had brought with them—Gary.

Fortunately, the feds had left Gary, allowing the pair to meet and for Rudy to woo him.

Rudy had more self-control than I do. No way can I wait.

Plus, Alpha Kontra was having the fae warrior, Prudhoe, look into the minds of the two humans—his mate and another man with similar coloring, although his features were much harder.

Can't let them harm my mate.

With the need to get his mate to safety being his only thought, Donovan pounded into the clearing. He wrapped his trunk around the sweet-smelling human's body, finding it slender and toned beneath the worn clothing. When Alpha

Kontra asked him if the human was his mate, Donovan bobbed his head in confirmation before turning and heading back into the swamp.

To Donovan's pleasure, his human didn't struggle in his hold. When he reached a small secluded area amidst the cypress trees, he came to a stop. Donovan carefully settled his human on his feet, but the man began to crumple.

Donovan rumbled softly, distress filling him upon realizing his mate had fainted. He carefully lay the male on the ground. Petting the tip of his trunk along the human's neck, Donovan felt a bit of relief upon finding the pulse there was steady and strong.

The snap of a branch followed by the scent of hyena and wolf on the breeze told him he was being followed. He searched the trees. A few seconds later, he spotted both. To his relief, both shifters were sitting some distance away, clearly not planning to intervene unless necessary.

Good.

His human stirring at his feet drew Donovan's attention. He saw the man's limbs twitch a little before he shifted restlessly. His mate rolled to his back. Lifting his hand to his head, he moaned softly as he rubbed at his temple and forehead.

A second later, the human's eyes snapped open. He peered up at Donovan with wide, shock-filled hazel eyes. His thin lips were parted in obvious disbelief.

"Holy shit," his human hissed.

Then he began crab-walking backward . . . until his back hit a cypress trunk. He glanced left and right.

Donovan knew his mate was searching for somewhere to escape, and distress filled him. Needing to soothe the human, he rumbled a soft vocalization as he took a step toward him. Resting the tip of his trunk on his mate's jeans-clad calf, Donovan petted up and down the leanly muscled limb.

The human tensed. He glanced from Donovan's petting to his face, then back to his petting. Nibbling his bottom lip, he furrowed his brows.

The scents of fear and shock gave way to confusion.

Okay. That's a bit of an improvement.

Donovan continued his gentle ministrations as he took in the human Fate had deemed the other half of his soul. With his mate sitting on the ground, he would guess him to be in the neighborhood of five-foot-ten or eleven. He had his dirty-blond hair caught in a short tail at his nape, accentuating his widow's peak. A number of strands of hair had escaped his tie to wave around his face, and Donovan gave in to the urge to use his trunk to gently tuck the ones on the left behind the human's ear.

Longing to do that with his fingers — to be able to trace along the slender column of the man's neck, to lick and nibble everywhere he touched — for the first time since before he'd been captured by witches, Donovan felt his human form stir within him. He gasped as the change began to tingle through him. His body felt an uncomfortable wave of fiery pain course through his bloodstream, and he barely managed to swallow his bugle of agony as his knees buckled.

Donovan barely heard the human's, "Holy shit!" over the sounds of his muscles popping and his bones cracking. The pain of his body shifting forced him to curl his newly forming fingers into fists, leaving him unable to reach for his mate. Even as Donovan wished he could soothe his human, he knew there was nothing he could do as his body shuddered and jolted through the most agonizing change of his life.

When Donovan finally peeled open his eyelids, he had to blink several times to get his eyes to focus. It took every bit of self-control he could muster to tip his head up. His mate wasn't where he'd been when Donovan's shift had started.

Oh, damn. Did he run?

"Relax, buddy." Vail's deep voice drew Donovan's attention. "Everything is fine. You're safe. Just take a few deep breaths."

Donovan turned toward Vail and did his best to control his sudden urge of possessive rage. His body trembled with his desire to stalk over there and yank a naked Vail away from his newly found mate. With a slow deep breath, Donovan reminded himself that Vail was a mated shifter, and he sure as hell would never be tempted to step out on his partner—Draven.

Besides, looking at the pair objectively, Donovan knew that Vail was trying to soothe his clearly freaked-out mate.

"Shit," Donovan rasped. "I didn't—" His voice failed him.

Donovan swallowed around his dry throat, trying to gain some moisture into his throat. It didn't work. His tongue felt thick and swollen. His attention slid to the murky swamp water to his right, and he wondered if his exhausted, aching limbs were strong enough to drag him to its edge.

To Donovan's relief, he didn't have to find out.

"Hey, elephant," Vail murmured, drawing Donovan's attention. "Just hang on a sec, kay, man? Payson's going to get Eli and some others. We'll help you and your mate."

Dipping his head in the slightest of nods, Donovan rested his cheek on the back of his hand. He stared longingly at his mate. He managed to slide his other hand toward his human, but he wasn't close enough to touch.

Vail seemed to understand. The wolf shifter was on one knee while sitting next to Donovan's human. He had his closer leg cocked up, hiding his groin in a poor attempt at covering his nudity. The wolf shifter rested one hand on the human's thigh. His other hand rubbed up and down his back, appearing to encourage the man to keep his head between his upturned knees in an obvious attempt to help him breathe and calm down.

"How ya doin' there, buddy?" Vail asked, his voice sounding low and gentle. "You ready to tell us your name?"

The human lifted his head just a little, but it was enough

for Donovan to meet the man's widely-dilated eyes. He forced a tremulous smile of his own, his lips struggling with the movement. Donovan hoped it was enough as he held the man's gaze.

"W-What—" The man paused and licked his lips, his brows furrowing. He glanced toward Vail and must have realized he was nude, too, for his cheeks darkened fetchingly. Donovan's mate focused on the ground. "What's going on?" Then he pinned Vail with a side-eyed look. "Are you a Rougarou?"

Vail's brows furrowed, and it was the wolf's turn to look confused. "Rougarou?"

Recognizing the term, Donovan registered his mate's Cajun accent. "Rougarou," he mumbled roughly. After another swallow, he managed, "Cajun legend about werewolves or shifters."

His human nodded slowly, even as he peered at Donovan through his lashes.

"Oh." Vail grinned as he barked a soft laugh. "Well, guess the legends had to come from somewhere." With a smirk curving his lips, he nodded. "I suppose that's an apt description." Then Vail shrugged and added, "Of course, I don't know the Rougarou legend, so I couldn't tell you how we differ from the stories."

"Wow," the young man whispered, slowly bringing his arms around his knees and straightening a little. Cocking his head, he stared at Donovan. "But you were an elephant. So . . . not a Rougarou?"

Donovan felt a measure of relief when Vail answered. "I think the legend of the Rougarou is an offshoot of what shifters really are," Vail claimed, patting his back. "A shifter can share his spirit with creatures other than a wolf." He pointed his index finger at Donovan. "In his case, an African elephant." Using a thumb to indicate over his shoulder, in the general direction of the Victorian, Vail declared, "There are dozens of different kinds of shifters back there."

"Like hyenas," Payson cut in, appearing from between the trees. He grinned widely as he sauntered forward. "I brought the doc." With a waggle of his brows, Payson held up a couple of pairs of jogging shorts. "Hopefully, one of these will fit ya. Wasn't certain what size you'd need." He dropped both beside Donovan's hip. Then he tossed a pair of cargo shorts at Vail before crouching next to Donovan's head — thank the gods he was wearing cargo shorts, too. "So, what's your name, man?"

"D-Donovan," he answered gruffly.

"Nice to meet you, Donovan," Eli greeted, lowering to a knee beside his hips, resting a black bag next to him. "But why don't we wait on having you answer any more questions until after I assess you. Hmm?"

Donovan nodded, liking that idea. He felt wrung out in a way he'd never experienced before. Every instinct screamed at him to crawl over to his human and cradle him in his lap, but his limbs just wouldn't cooperate.

"I'll start with a gentle wipe-down as Eli tests your muscles," Sam told him. Eli's small, wolf shifter partner smiled at him as he pulled a damp cloth from the bag. "And Payson can ask your mate a few questions."

"Okay," Donovan murmured, turning his attention to his human as Payson approached him. He tensed slightly as the enforcer drew near him, only to relax again when Payson settled on his ass off to the side and crossed his legs Indian-style.

Payson flashed Donovan a knowing look before refocusing on the human. "So, what's your name, man?" Resting his forearms on his thighs, he added bluntly, "And why were ya shootin' at Vail and Sam here?"

Glancing between the pair that Payson indicated, his mate sucked in a sharp breath. "I-I d-didn't." He even swayed a little as his breath came in short gasps.

"He's telling the truth, Payson," Vail stated, shaking his head as he once again rubbed his back. "It was his asshole partner." Sweeping his gaze over Donovan's mate, the wolf shifter eyed him with a speculative gleam in his eyes. "Let me guess. The dude's your older brother, and he likes to drag you into trouble." Then his eyes narrowed. "Or do you look up to him and are trying to emulate him and make him proud?"

"No! Absolutely not," his mate countered. "I would never poach if he didn't —" Grimacing, his face fell. "But if I don't —"

Once again, his words seemed to fail him.

"Okay, guys. Stop freaking the poor guy out." Yuma, a small penguin shifter, had arrived. He gave both Vail and Payson scolding looks as he settled on his knees before Donovan's mate. "Okay. Let's try this again." Yuma reached forward and took one of his mate's hands between his own. "I'm Yuma. These yahoos are Vail and Payson." Tipping his chin toward Donovan and those with him, he added, "Eli's the doc. Sam is his nurse as well as his partner. And I hear the elephant is Donovan." Yuma glanced at him and winked. "Congrats, by the way." Then he refocused on the human. "So, what's your name?"

Chapter Three

Oh my god! I've been caught by a tribe of Rougarou!
While Horace had always been fascinated by the tales of men with the ability to turn into wolves, never in a million years had he thought they could be true.

Realizing he didn't have a choice, Horace peered at the small man holding his hand. "Horace Broussard." When Yuma squeezed his hand in encouragement, he murmured, "And, yeah, Herbert's my brother, but I don't look up to him." Rubbing the back of his neck with his free hand, he admitted, "It's just . . . if I don't do what I'm told, he, uh, well, he . . ." Horace bit his lower lip, unable to admit those words. Instead, he whispered, "He's a bully."

"Ah." As Yuma nodded, his one-word response seemed to say so much—as if he completely understood what Horace wasn't saying. "Well, we certainly aren't going to let him do that to you anymore." Yuma smiled brightly at him. "Are you gay?"

Upon hearing the blunt question, Horace gaped.
Why would he ask that? Could he somehow tell?
Fear slithered down his spine for a new reason.
If this Yuma guy can tell, does that mean Herbert could figure it out?

Horace couldn't imagine the beatings that would earn him. And he just knew that his brother would claim it was to make him a man. He'd heard his brother share his feelings on *cocksuckers* plenty of times when homosexuals came up in the news.

While much of the country—and a large portion of the world—was becoming more accepting, Herbert and his crowd were definitely not.

"Oh, wow." Yuma squeezed Horace's hand. "I'm so sorry, Horace. I didn't mean to freak you out." When Horace focused on Yuma, the small, slender man sported a reassuring smile. "We're all gay or bisexual here, so you're in safe company. I promise."

His jaw sagging open, Horace glanced around at the other gathered men. Sam smiled, Vail nodded, and Payson waggled his eyebrows. Eli remained focused on whatever he was doing to Donovan.

When Horace finally focused on the man who'd stolen him from the scary guys, he couldn't help but notice the heat in the guy's deep gray eyes. While he'd never been on the receiving end of such a look from a guy before, he recognized it. The big man sprawled on his stomach was attracted to him.

Wow. Why?

Horace didn't understand that. He didn't think he was much to look at. His pronounced widow's peak made his face look too narrow. The bump left behind after his broken nose healed took away any chance of even being considered remotely cute. On top of that, Herbert took most of the money he eared, so the clothes he bought from a local secondhand store were threadbare and baggy on his too-slender frame.

"We have so much explaining to do," Vail stated, patting him on the back. "Come on. Let's go back to the house. It's more comfortable." When Vail's stomach growled, he added, "And I'm ready for a meal. Running always makes me work up an appetite."

To Horace's embarrassment, his stomach rumbled, too. Evidently, his bacon and eggs had worn off.

Payson cackled as he rose to his feet. "Come on, man." He held out his hand, palm up. "We'll feed ya, explain shifters, mates, and hot sex." Waggling his eyebrows, Payson cut a glance Donovan's way before refocusing on Horace. "And this is the first time Donovan's been in human form for years, so you can bet that once he gets his strength back, he'll be ready to rock your world for days."

"Payson." Eli stated the other man's name in clear warning. "Do try not to freak out the human. Hmm?"

Horace felt his cheeks heat, and he nibbled his bottom lip. As Payson cackled again, Horace took his hand, allowing the other man to pull him to his feet, and he cut a look toward Donovan. The man continued to stare at him, but his expression appeared tempered by concern.

Too bad. I liked the attraction better.

With a sigh, Horace tugged his hand from Payson's hold once he was on his own two feet. He wrapped his arms around his waist. As he allowed Yuma and Vail to begin urging him back the way the elephant had come, he peered over his shoulder at the others.

Gasping, Horace watched as Eli slid his arms under Donovan's large frame. The man rose to his six-foot-five height, and he barely looked to be straining. As Eli strode forward, Horace couldn't resist taking a visual sweep of Donovan's body.

Finding himself entranced, Horace froze. He admired Donovan's broad shoulders and thickly muscled limbs. The extra weight he carried around the middle as a small spare tire did nothing to detract from his appeal.

And, oh, wow. Look at his cock.

Horace had never seen another man's naked dick in real life. While Vail had been sitting nude beside him, he'd positioned his body in a way where Horace hadn't glimpsed it. Of course, he hadn't tried to look, either. Horace hadn't been attracted to the wiry, dark-haired male.

Donovan, though. Wow!

As Horace stared, he noticed the thick piece of meat at the juncture of Donovan's thighs twitched and began to swell. He sucked in a surprised breath, wondering what it would look like completely hard. Horace bet the heavy balls underneath would feel so good in his palm. Would Donovan let him—

"Mind out of the gutter while I'm carrying Donovan," Eli barked, scowling at him. "If you want to ogle him, come to the house and help him with a shower."

Horace felt his cheeks go up in flames. Ducking his head, he hunched his shoulders and started hustling toward Yuma and Vail, who had paused a dozen or so feet away from him. He glanced at them from beneath his lashes, but he couldn't meet their gazes.

"Don't give my mate shit for admiring me," Donovan muttered softly. "He should never be made to feel embarrassed by his desire for me."

"Yeah, well, he can express his desire when I'm not carrying you, asshole," Eli snapped, his voice full of annoyance. "I don't need to see your wang waving in the air with every step I take."

Hearing those words made Horace's blush creep all the way up into his ears.

Oh, god. Maybe a hole will appear and swallow me.

"Here we go," Sam murmured from behind them. "All fixed." Then he scolded, "And it's never okay to shame mates, Eli. You know that."

Growling softly, Eli called, "My apologies, Horace. I should have chosen a different way to express my discomfort at holding an aroused male who is not my partner."

"It's okay," Horace quickly replied with a glance over his shoulder. Sam's fix appeared to be one of the shorts Payson had brought draped over Donovan's groin. Realizing he was staring once more, Horace jerked his attention forward again. "Um." His mind went blank . . . until he spotted the Victorian amidst the trees and the men milling about. Horace's attention landed on the black man who'd helped him out of the boat, and he recalled scary guy number one and Yuma's words. "A-All these guys are gay?" After a second of hesitation, Horace added, "Or bisexual?"

"Yeppers," Yuma responded, sliding his arm around one of Horace's own, maybe as a show of support. "And we're all open about it. You'll see plenty of guys kissing and the occasional groping."

Waggling his brows, Payson stated glibly, "I love sitting around with my man, Land, and watching the show." He snickered. "It's almost like watching soft porn. Great foreplay."

Horace blushed even more, although he didn't know how his cheeks could get any hotter. Somehow, they did. He peered away from the others in time to see the scary dude appear, striding around the side of the house.

Freezing, Horace felt a wash of fear crash over him when the guy snapped his attention to his group exiting the trees.

"Hey, it's okay," Yuma assured, tugging him forward once more. "That's Alpha Kontra, our leader." His voice lowered until he whispered, "I know he looks like a mean badass, but he's really a big soft teddy bear."

Payson snorted, striding past them. "You mean if you're family, he's a big soft teddy bear." With an eye roll, he declared, "But you try to hurt any of his people, better run far, far away and pray he never catches ya."

"Payson," Yuma scolded. "Seriously?" He rested his free hand on his hip as he scowled at Payson. "I'm trying to relax him here."

Pausing, Payson turned and looked at them. His brows were furrowed, and he looked beyond confused. "By lying to him?" Payson rolled his eyes. "That ain't the way to relax a guy."

"I never intended to hurt any of his, uh, people," Horace quickly stated, glancing between them. "I wished I never pointed out the wolves to Herbert. I was just so surprised."

With a deep sigh, Horace mumbled, "I should know better than that by now."

"Well, now that you're with us, you won't have to worry about your meanie brother anymore," Yuma declared, his black brows furrowing into a frown. "You're with us now, so that makes you family."

"How does that work?" Horace asked absently, too busy watching Eli stride ahead of them. The guy who'd helped him from the boat opened the front door for Eli, allowing him to disappear into the large home.

Vail touched Horace's chin, urging him to meet his gaze. "That means" — the man's brown eyes held a warm glow of understanding — "it's time for us to make a meal and explain shifters and mating to you while we eat." Cocking his head, Vail told him, "I'm glad you don't look up to your brother because I have a feeling we're going to have to exorcise him from your life."

"Really?" Horace gaped at Vail. As much as he didn't want to admit it, he would really, *really* like that. Still . . . Horace knew how persistent his brother could be. "I've tried to get away from him before," he admitted, rubbing the back of his neck as a different kind of embarrassment filled him. "He and his buddies never let me get far. I'm, like, his servant, and he won't want to lose the guy who cooks and cleans for him. Plus, he takes most of my money."

As ashamed as Horace felt because of how he let his brother treat him, he couldn't see his way out of it.

"Because now" — the huge bruiser who'd easily forced Herbert to drop his gun into the pond appeared next to them — "you have a whole hell of a lot of help."

Yuma grinned. "Hey, Sam." Pointing at the house, he told the other man, "Eli already took Donovan into the house. That's the elephant's name."

The man with the scar nodded once.

21

Continuing, Yuma told the dark-haired male, "And this is Horace. We're going to go feed him and tell him all about shifters and mates." Turning to Horace, Yuma told him, "This is Sam Abbott. He's our pack's beta, so if you need anything, just let him know, and he'll take care of it."

Even as Horace nodded, he couldn't imagine going to Sam Abbott for anything. The man didn't appear to have an approachable bone in his body.

Still, his nod seemed to be all Yuma was looking for, since he stated, "I smell steaks. Let's go see if they're ready."

"Sounds good," Sam rumbled, turning to fall into step with them. "I can always go for a steak."

As Horace followed Yuma's urging and began moving toward the Victorian with the other men, he found his mouth starting to water.

He couldn't remember the last time he'd had a steak.

CHAPTER FOUR

Eli sighed deeply after settling Donovan on the chair Sam had placed in the shower.

Donovan smirked. "You didn't want anyone to know you were struggling," he murmured, keeping his voice low for a couple of reasons.

First off, even after drinking an entire bottle of water provided by Sam, Donovan's throat still felt rough. Secondly, Donovan knew the dominant snake shifter wouldn't appreciate his weakness being broadcasted to anyone else in the pack. To that end, he spoke softly because the doors appeared to be thin.

"I know I'm not light," Donovan continued, noticing Eli's eyes narrow just a smidge. He shrugged one shoulder and pointed out, "I'm an elephant. We require a little extra weight in our human form, too."

Eli scoffed as he reached over and turned on the water. "Yeah. Thanks for keeping that on the down-low." He glanced over his shoulder, probably to make certain his mate was still on the other side of the door fetching fresh towels and clothes for Donovan. "I never want my mate to think of me as weak." To Donovan's surprise, Eli's cheeks actually took on just the slightest shade of pink. "Let's just say, when we first met, I ended up ill and put my foot in my mouth." The dominant shifter grimaced as he admitted, "Had to work hard to get past that, and I never want either of us to end up back there again."

Donovan didn't understand the dominant and submissive

relationship that the pair practiced, but he would never judge another for enjoying that lifestyle, either. What worked for one couple might not work for another and vice versa. To that end, Donovan judged a person on their character.

"I'll never mention it to another," Donovan promised. After all, he hated how weak he was at that moment. As a shifter, he wasn't at all shy, so sitting in front of Eli nude wasn't the issue. Instead, it was how difficult Donovan found it to reach out and pick up the washcloth. Groaning softly, he muttered, "Gods, why are my muscles so tired and sore?"

"Because you haven't used them in . . . how many years?" Sam answered as he entered the bathroom. He quickly shut the door behind him before placing a bundle of items on the bathroom counter. The slender black man offered him a sweet smile. "How many years has it been since you were in human form?"

Donovan blinked a few times, considering that. "What year did you say it was again?" He knew he'd heard it once or twice in passing while in elephant form, but he wanted to confirm. Upon hearing Sam's answer, Donovan sighed deeply. "Over twenty-six years," he murmured, wondering how he'd lost track of so much time. "Twenty-seven years come this Thanksgiving."

"Damn," Eli muttered from where he'd settled on the closed lid of the toilet. Crossing his arms over his chest, he shook his head. "Did you get taken by the witches over the holiday? Why on earth wouldn't your herd have registered you as missing?"

Scoffing, Donovan didn't bother commenting when Sam, having stripped to his shorts, stepped into the shower and plucked the wash cloth from his limp hand. "Because at that point, I didn't have a herd."

Sam growled softly under his breath. "Damn. How did

these witches always seem to know how to target lone shifters?"

Donovan would never say it out loud, but he thought the small black wolf shifter's growls were damn cute. Instead, he shook his head. "Wasn't a lone elephant," he admitted, his anger surging, as impotent as it was. "Had a boyfriend. He sold me out."

Freezing in his cleaning ministrations, Sam gaped at him.

"Oh, fuck," Eli snarled, curling his lip. "Who the hell is he?" The anaconda shifter leaned toward him, his eyes narrowing with deadly intent. "We'll track him down for you." With a cold smile creasing his features, Eli told him, "If you want him brought to you for shifter justice, it will be done. Otherwise—" He allowed the sentence to hang.

Donovan understood. One way or another, all Donovan had to do was give his ex's name. Sooner or later, these guys would take him out.

He even understood why they would do it, too. Shifter justice was clear. He knew about paranormals. When his ex had sold him out to witches, his crimes had fallen under the paranormal purview.

That means I get to exact shifter justice.

Except, all that was completely unnecessary.

With a dark satisfaction filling him, Donovan began reaching for the cloth the frozen Sam still held. His movements must have brought the wolf shifter out of his shock. The submissive male quickly returned to his duties as a nurse—caring for his patient.

Donovan even understood why Eli remained in the room. The male didn't want his mate in the room alone with a naked man. It didn't matter that Donovan could hardly move or that Sam would never want him. No, it was all about Eli's nature to care for his mate.

Someday, I'll have that with Horace.

"Well?" Eli prodded. "How about it?" His eyes narrowed.

25

"Don't tell me you're still willing to protect him after what happened to you."

Scoffing darkly, Donovan rolled his head, ignoring the way Sam worked the washcloth up his leg to the crease of his groin. "No," he replied softly. He curved his lip into a cold smile. "Can't protect a dead man."

"Dead man?" Eli cocked his head as he narrowed his eyes. "You sure?"

"Oh, very sure," Donovan confirmed, holding Eli's gaze steadily. "Killed him myself."

Sam snapped his gaze to him, even as he continued to work the cloth over Donovan's arm. "Really?" he questioned with wide eyes. "How?"

While Donovan didn't think Sam really wanted specifics—he guessed the question had been a knee-jerk reaction—from the narrowing of Eli's eyes, the snake shifter definitely wanted to know.

After casting a small smile Sam's way, Donovan met Eli's gaze. "The witches brought him to my cage to gloat." He tipped his face into the falling shower water, sliding his eyelids closed, enjoying the warmth as he thought of that cold, dark day. "They didn't have me as sedated as they thought they did," Donovan murmured, recalling his ex's curled lips and disgusted sneer. "He didn't leave the elephant habitat alive that day."

When the human had called Donovan an abomination—something his ex-lover had claimed his family had called him when he'd come out and was rejected by them—Donovan had snapped. He'd gathered enough energy to swing his head and snap out his trunk. His huge appendage had struck his ex across his torso. The human had screamed as he careened across the room. His head had slammed into the concrete wall with a sickening—and final—crunch before the human had slumped to the floor in a pool of his own blood.

Seconds later, Donovan had been blasted by a couple of sleep spells as well as several tranquilizer darts. His legs had given out, and he'd crashed to the floor, unconsciousness taking him as he watched several witches rushing to his ex's side. Donovan hadn't been certain he'd kill his ex until one of the witches had let it slip several days later. She'd been warning the acolyte she'd been training to clean his cage to always be on her guard and never take his docility for granted.

Eli hummed, drawing Donovan's attention. Upon seeing the snake shifter's narrowed eyes, he couldn't help arching one brow in silent challenge. The corners of the dominant male's lips twitched a little.

"Will you have a problem with the fact that your mate is human?" Eli asked bluntly.

Closing his eyes, Donovan relaxed into a silent Sam's ministration as the shifter washed his hair. "No," he answered softly. "My mate is a gift from Fate." Easing his eyelids open, Donovan fixed Eli with a hard stare. "My ex shouldn't have known about shifters. I didn't know he did or that he felt like that about us." With a snort as he thought about Horace, Donovan couldn't imagine two more different men. "I don't know how he figured me out, but I know that Horace is not the same. Just his reactions to learning that we're different and his acceptance of the Rougarou told me that."

Eli nodded. "Fair enough." He turned his attention to Sam. "You about done, my mate?"

Sam urged Donovan to tip his head back so he could rinse the conditioner out of his hair and beard one last time. "Just about," the nurse replied. "What do you want done with your hair and beard?" Easing out of the shower, Sam grabbed a towel and began drying himself as he told him, "Zhaul, the panda shifter, is really good at giving haircuts and shaves. If you want, I can go get him for you."

Donovan lifted a heavy hand and threaded his fingers

through his hair. Then he ran them over his shaggy beard. In the past, Donovan hadn't needed to shave often, but after spending over twenty-five years as an elephant without the opportunity to shave, he'd ended up with quite the shaggy facial hair.

"If Zhaul has time, I'd appreciate that," Donovan admitted. "I'll just have him trim up my hair so I can pull it into a decent ponytail, but I'd really prefer a goatee instead of a beard."

Sam nodded as he handed a towel to Eli. "I'll track him down and ask while you dry Donovan and get him into the shorts I brought," the wolf shifter stated, smiling at his partner.

"Of course, my mate," Eli confirmed. Dipping his head, he pecked a kiss to Sam's wet lips. "Put on some dry shorts before you find Zhaul."

"Yes, sir," Sam murmured, smiling lovingly at Eli. Then he slipped from the room.

Eli placed a foot in the shower and proceeded to dry and assist Donovan with dressing.

It didn't take long for Sam to return with Zhaul. "Hey, Donovan. Congrats on shifting." The big panda shifter smiled as he held out his hand.

"Thanks," Donovan replied, shaking the other shifter's hand. "I know it's because I met my mate."

"Well, hopefully, the mates for the rest of the guys show up soon." As Donovan murmured his agreement, Zhaul spread a towel on the floor. "To catch your hair," he explained. Then he and Eli moved the chair and Donovan with it, onto the towel. "So, what do you want done?" Zhaul asked, eyeing him somewhat critically.

After Donovan explained, Zhaul nodded and got to work. He ended up being just as skilled as Sam had claimed. In short order, Donovan's steel-gray hair was trimmed and pulled away from his face, and his whiskers were shaved into a goatee.

"What do you think?" Zhaul indicated the mirror hanging over the sink.

Donovan stared at his reflection and smiled faintly. He was more tanned than he'd ever been in his life, but that made sense. He'd spent nearly the last twenty-seven years outside. His features were a little narrower, too, telling him he was still a smidge under his ideal weight.

Considering all the food the guys were always preparing, Donovan didn't think it would be long before he packed it back on. He hoped it would be muscle, too. When Zhaul shifted his weight nervously, Donovan returned his attention to the panda shifter.

"This is great. Thank you, Zhaul."

Zhaul beamed. "You're welcome." Then he exited with a wave, saying, "See you around."

"Come on, Donovan," Eli encouraged, sliding his arm around his shoulders. "Let's get you settled in bed. Then we'll bring you a meal." Eli helped Donovan find his feet for the first time in human form and helped him slowly make his way out of the bathroom. "I know you're an elephant, which is an herbivore, but I'm assuming you eat meat while in human form?"

"I do," Donovan confirmed. The smell of the grilling steaks tantalized his senses, and his mouth watered. "If you don't mind, I'd love one of those steaks that Yuma mentioned."

"Absolutely," Eli agreed with a satisfied nod. "The protein will help your muscles recover more swiftly."

"Great." Donovan didn't think anything sounded better. "Thanks, doc."

Eli nodded as he helped Donovan settle in a bedroom, his back to the headboard with pillows propping him up.

"Hey, Donovan," Sam greeted, entering the room. "Look who I found?"

Donovan's attention was riveted to the man who followed Sam. "Hi, Horace."

To his pleasure, Horace offered him a shy, tentative smile, and it was the sweetest expression Donovan had ever seen.

"Hi," Horace murmured. Lifting the plate he carried, he told him, "The guys downstairs helped me prepare a plate of food for you." Horace peered at Donovan from beneath his lashes as a hint of pink entered his cheeks. "I-I hope that's okay."

"More than." Donovan patted the mattress beside him. "Will you join me?"

Then Donovan waited with bated breath, hope and anticipation filling him.

CHAPTER FIVE

After a few seconds of hesitation, Horace nodded his agreement. He crossed to the bed and placed the dish on the nightstand. Horace glanced Eli's way, and the doc gave him the slightest of nods of permission.

Horace carefully climbed onto the bed. Settling with his back to the headboard, he stuffed the pillow Eli offered him behind his back. Once Horace was settled, Donovan reached over and gently took his hand, threading their fingers together.

"Thank you for joining me, Horace," Donovan rumbled, turning a little on the bed to focus on him fully.

While Donovan's deep voice remained soft, it no longer sounded painfully raspy.

"Are you feeling a little better?" Horace asked, trying to ignore the way goose bumps erupted on his arm from the contact. "You sound better."

"A hot shower and shave did wonders," Donovan told him, using his thumb to rub over the back of Horace's hand, causing tingles to travel up his flesh. "That meal you brought smells amazing. Will you eat with me?"

Horace swallowed hard, trying to get moisture into his suddenly dry throat. "I-I ate downstairs with, um, some of the others," he admitted. Glancing at Donovan with a side-eyed look, he told the man, "They, um, they explained a lot to me."

"Did they?" Donovan indicated the plate, finally releasing his hand. "Why don't you give me the highlights while I eat?"

Nodding, Horace quickly removed the lid from the platter

before picking it up and moving it to Donovan's lap. The silverware had been under the dome, so the big man quickly picked them up. Donovan hummed as he slid the fork through the hill of mashed potatoes and gravy.

"Looks amazing," Donovan murmured before easing the fork into his mouth. He moaned softly, his eyelids sliding to half-mast. "Gods, forgot how good this could taste." Donovan immediately scooped up more and slid it into his mouth, letting out another soft, appreciative grunt.

"Sounds like someone likes it," Sam teased as he set a tray with several drinks on the nightstand closer to Donovan. Donovan replied only with a grunt. Chuckling, Sam pointed to the tray. "Black coffee, but there's sugar and creamer packets if you want them. There's also orange juice, tea, and lemonade. I can get you just about anything else, too." Sam turned and smiled at Horace. "Would you like a drink while you sit and talk?"

"Um, sure?" Horace replied.

Donovan swallowed, then smiled at Horace. "Are you asking Sam or telling him?" he teased. Leaning over, he bumped his shoulder into Horace's. "And what would you like, sweetheart?"

"Sweetheart?" Horace couldn't help but repeat. He felt his cheeks heat, but it was due more to pleasure than embarrassment. When Donovan just smiled at him, Horace admitted, "N-Never had anyone call me an endearment before."

Donovan's full lips tipped into a sad-looking smile. "I'm sorry to hear that, but I'm glad I get to be the one to change it." Then he picked up his knife and indicated the large T-bone steak on his plate. "You sure you don't want any of this?"

Horace shook his head, unable to keep back his smile. "I'm glad you get to change it, too."

With a large bite of steak hovering over his plate on his

fork, Donovan asked, "Even with the changes that I'm sure the shifters downstairs explained to you?"

Blowing out a slow breath, Horace admitted, "I'll be grateful for most of those changes." Then he sobered and admitted, "Although, I'm not certain how your people will actually accomplish certain things."

"What do you mean?" Donovan shook his head and, setting down his knife, lifted his forefinger in a hold-on gesture. "Would you like one of these drinks here?" Then Donovan leaned close and sniffed at him. With a smirk, he added, "Or maybe you'd like another glass of whatever wine you were drinking."

Unable to help himself, Horace felt his face heat. He hunched his shoulders and winced. "Um, you can smell that?"

Donovan nodded once, looking confused. "Shifter sense of smell," he stated simply. Placing his fork on the plate, he slid his fingers around Horace's. "And now it's telling me that you scent of unease and embarrassment." After squeezing his fingers lightly, Donovan asked, "Why would me knowing you had a glass of wine embarrass you?"

Horace grimaced. "Wine isn't a manly drink," he whispered, glancing at him side-eyed before refocusing on his jeans. "Um, you're a big guy. Didn't know if you'd approve."

"Anything that makes you happy will make me happy," Donovan claimed in a quiet, sure voice. "Well." He winced. "Unless it's dangerous. Can't say I'd be the happiest about you wanting to wrestle crocodiles or something."

Scoffing, Horace felt relief begin to soothe him. "Uh, no. Don't particularly want to do that."

Donovan nodded. "Good." Turning his attention to Sam, he requested, "Can you find out from the guys downstairs what kind of wine Horace was drinking and bring him a glass, please?"

33

Sam nodded. "Will do." Reaching the door, he paused and peered over his shoulder at them. "You want anything other than what's on that tray?"

Scoffing softly, Donovan told him, "I'd love a beer. A dark brew, if you have it, but anything is fine."

Chuckling, Sam nodded. "Just want to enjoy the flavor after so long, huh?"

"Exactly." Donovan winced as he glanced at the tray of drinks. "And I'll keep the orange juice and tea." He met Horace's gaze. "I'm not a fan of coffee. You want it?"

Horace wrinkled his nose. "Uh, no, thank you."

Donovan chuckled. "Not a fan, either?"

Shaking his head, Horace noticed Sam grinning as he left. "I'll drink it first thing in the morning during the week because I always have to get up early to make Herbert's breakfast, but—" Horace paused, nibbling his bottom lip. "God, if I try to move in here with you, he's gonna cause trouble."

"He won't know where you are," Alpha Kontra stated as he strode into the room. He tipped his beer bottle at Donovan's plate. "Eat up, or Eli will have my hide."

Horace bit back a snicker, having a hard time imagining that. While still a little uncomfortable with the big man's presence—he'd chatted with him a little downstairs—he was no longer scared of the guy. Learning that Kontra transformed into a grizzly bear should have freaked him out, but instead, he found it sort of reassured him.

After all, with Kontra being a badass bear, maybe he really could get away from Herbert's influence.

Donovan resumed eating, murmuring, "Yes, Alpha."

Kontra grabbed the straight-backed chair set in front of the desk and dragged it toward the bed. After spinning it around, he straddled it backward. He placed his forearms on the back, allowing the beer bottle to dangle between his fingers.

"So, you're open to bonding with Donovan, Horace," Kontra began without preamble. As Horace felt his face heat, the big male chuckled softly. "You'll get used to how open we are about certain needs." Kontra shrugged his huge shoulders. "And sex between mates is pretty much a biological imperative. It helps build your bond, but it doesn't replace talking in building a relationship."

"O-Okay," Horace stuttered. Lifting his knees, he wrapped his arms around them. "Um, never been in a relationship," he admitted, glancing between the men. Realizing he had to bite the bullet, so to speak, he blew out a breath before admitting, "Look, Herbert is a bigot, and he's been ruling my life since our parents died when I was fifteen. Herbert was nineteen, and he moved back home. Said it was to take care of me, but it was really because the house was paid for." With a wince and a half-shrug, Horace added, "Plus, then he could have free labor with, well, everything."

"That stops now," Donovan growled around his bite of steak.

"How?" Horace didn't really intend to counter the man, but he just didn't get it. "He's not going to just let me go."

"He won't have a choice, Horace," Kontra told him, tapping his forefinger on his bottle. "You're an adult."

Horace sighed deeply, his shoulders sagging. "That doesn't matter to him."

He glanced at Donovan, but he didn't want to interrupt his eating — doctor's orders, after all. Instead, Horace focused on Kontra. Considering he was the leader, he needed to be warned of what might be coming.

"I mentioned moving in with a friend when I was nineteen," Horace told the bear shifter. "Herbert beat me so bad I was pissing blood for several days." Donovan growled and wrapped his arm around his shoulders, tucking him against his side protectively. Horace snuggled against him, enjoying the support as he continued, "When I was well enough to tell my friend, I was hoping he would help me leave town, his apartment was empty, and he was gone." Rubbing his forehead, Horace admitted, "I never did find out what happened to him, but Herbert's friend, Walter, claimed that he'd moved out of town."

"Tell us his name, and I'll have my people look into him," Kontra told him, frowning.

Horace nodded. "Joey LaFleur. Uh, Josiah LaFleur." Rubbing his shin with on hand, he added, "If they paid him to leave, I don't want to know about it. I just want to know he's okay, and his body wasn't tossed in the swamp somewhere."

"You think your brother is capable of that?" Alpha Kontra asked sharply.

Shrugging again, Horace whispered, "I wish I could say no, but . . . I think so." He hesitated a second, then told them, "A couple of years ago, I worked at the local diner. I discreetly saved up my tips until I had a little over a thousand in cash." Horace picked at a frayed patch of his jeans. "I bought a bus ticket out of town, but one of Herbert's friends spotted me. He told my brother. He . . . I . . . ."

"You can tell us or not," Donovan crooned, nuzzling his temple with his newly trimmed goatee. "Know that either way, I will keep you safe."

Horace allowed his eyelids to slide closed. Enjoying the big man's gentle ministrations, he sighed. He didn't know why Donovan's touch felt so wonderful. Horace just knew that he wanted everything these people were offering him.

And that means they deserve the truth.

Opening his eyes, Horace smiled at Donovan before refocusing on Kontra. Before he could open his mouth, Sam reappeared with the wine and beer.

"Perfect timing, Sam," Kontra told the small male, who gave the alpha a bemused smile. With a shake of his head, he added, "Horace has a tough tale to share and could use a little liquid courage."

Sam winced as he handed Horace the wine. "Sorry to hear that." Then he placed the beer on the tray with the other drinks. "Do you need anything else?"

When Donovan shook his head, Horace did the same.

"Please shut the door behind you, Sam," Kontra rumbled, effectively dismissing the shifter.

Nodding, Sam exited the room.

Kontra took a swig of his beer, then refocused on Horace. "Whatever you want to tell us will only leave this room as necessary to keep my people safe."

Horace nodded before taking a sip of his wine. While he couldn't remember the label, he really liked the shiraz. After another sip, Horace forced himself to admit the rest.

CHAPTER SIX

K eeping his arm around Horace, Donovan polished off the rest of his food. He'd already cut his steak into bite-sized chunks, so he only needed the one hand. That meant he could hold Horace, soothing himself and his animal that his human was safe in his arms.

"When Herbert dragged me from the bus station, there was a deputy standing right there," Horace told them, a frown creasing his features. "He didn't do anything. When a tourist pointed it out, the deputy laughed and said it was just the Broussard brothers having a family squabble and to not worry about it."

"Damn," Kontra muttered. "Corrupt cops in town, too."

Horace nodded. "When we got home, the beating was bad. I ended up with a broken wrist," he told them, his voice quiet as he pressed even closer to Donovan. "Lost my job at the diner while healing, and now I work at the grocery store." Curling his lip, Horace grumbled, "No tips there."

"Herbert will never get near you again," Donovan declared, hating the disbelief he smelled in Horace's scent. One way or another, he would make good on his vow. "I promise, my mate." After setting his plate aside, Donovan cradled Horace's jaw, urging his human to meet his gaze. "I will protect you."

"This is where Herbert saw me last. He'll come back here looking for me," Horace whispered, worry furrowing his brow. "He'll bring his friends, and if that doesn't work, he'll bring the sheriff, claiming you're kidnapping me."

"He doesn't know where this place is," Kontra claimed, shaking his head. "We removed that knowledge from him."

Horace snapped his attention to Kontra. "Really? How?"

"Vail's mate, Draven, is a warlock-vampire hybrid," Kontra explained. "Vampires have the ability to alter the memories of most humans."

"They do?" Horace squeaked, revealing that vampires must have been touched on by the guys downstairs. "Holy shit."

Kontra chuckled, clearly amused by Donovan's mate's response. "Yep. It's how vampires can hide in plain sight. Can't have humans remembering that they've been sucked on, now can they?" With a reassuring grin, Kontra continued, "Anyway. Once Prudhoe saw what a self-entitled asshole Herbert was, we decided to remove his memory of being here. Herbert was returned to his boat, and we towed him out to a different area of the swamp. After giving him a bit of a knock on the head, when Herbert wakes, he'll think he was out there poaching by himself." With a smirk, Kontra added, "Herbert will think he got hit by a large gator, lost his balance, dropped his gun into the swamp, and knocked himself out for a while. When he goes home, he'll be none the wiser about us out here."

Horace nodded slowly, seeming to be processing that. "Okay. Um." He glanced between them again. "If he was poaching alone, what does he think I was doing?"

With a grin, Kontra waggled his eyebrows. "You spent the night at your boyfriend's house."

In seconds, the blood drained from Horace's face, leaving him deathly pale. He squeaked, breathing swiftly. The scent of his fear hit Donovan just as he realized his mate was having a panic attack.

"Shit, shit," Kontra muttered, moving swiftly toward the bed.

Donovan urged Horace's head between his upturned knees. "Breathe slow and deep, sweetheart." Rubbing up and down his side with one hand, he kept his other wrapped around his shoulder, keeping him close. "You're safe. You're totally safe. I gotcha." When Horace continued to whimper and shudder, Donovan snapped his attention to Kontra. "What do I do?"

"Let's put him on your lap sideways," Kontra instructed, helping him lift Horace. "Tuck his nose against your neck. Even as a human, your scent will help calm him." Putting deed to his instruction, Kontra helped him position Horace's face against his neck. "Keep holding him and talking to him." With a shake of his head, he murmured, "I'm sorry. Obviously, that was the wrong thing for us to do. We'll get it sorted. It'll be okay."

After several more minutes, Horace finally stopped trembling. His whimpers ceased. It took a little longer for his breathing to slow until he was taking long, deep breaths, clearly taking in Donovan's scent, just as Kontra had predicted.

"Okay," Kontra began softly, sitting on the side of the bed beside them. "We need to know what set you off, Horace." Reaching over, Kontra grabbed the glass of wine he'd taken from Horace's trembling hands before placing him on Donovan's lap. "Here. Take a couple of sips, and steady yourself. Then talk to us."

Horace eased his face away from Donovan's neck, but he didn't try to move off his lap. After taking the glass, he did as Kontra had bidden. He took a sip, then two, before cradling the stemware in one hand. Resting his shoulder against Donovan's chest, Horace sagged against him while gripping his upper arm with his free hand, clutching him as if he feared being forced away from Donovan.

Not happening.

"H-Herbert doesn't know I'm g-gay," Horace whispered,

as if finding it difficult to say the words out loud. "He's a . . . he's a bigot."

"Damn, I'm sorry, Horace." Kontra frowned as he shook his head. "I didn't mean to out you to him."

Unable to contain his curiosity, Donovan asked, "So, have you only dated women then?" A feral possessiveness began to seep through him at the idea of his mate having never been touched by another man.

"I-I-I've never, um, I've never dated anyone," Horace told him. Peering at Donovan through his lashes, he whispered, "I'm a virgin."

That feral possessiveness escaped him in a rumble of pleasure. "Oh, sweetheart," Donovan crooned gruffly. Sliding his hand up Horace's neck, he threaded his fingers into his hair. "I will take such good care of you."

Then Donovan began lowering his head, intending to seal his mouth over Horace's in a deep, plundering kiss.

Kontra cleared his throat, interrupting the moment. "Sorry, Donovan," he stated.

Donovan frowned at Kontra, thinking he certainly didn't look like he was sorry.

The corner of Kontra's lip twitched, telling Donovan that the alpha had probably caught on to what he was thinking. "Tell me what you think Herbert will try to do to you," he ordered softly. "You clearly think he's a bullying asshole. What should we expect?"

Yeah, I caught on to that, too.

Horace took a sip of wine, then a second one, perhaps to buy time to gather his thoughts. "Well." Rubbing his temple against Donovan's chest hair, he sighed deeply. "I . . . I'm not totally sure. If he thinks I'm gay, I can never go back to the house." Horace winced, his scent darkening with undertones of sadness. "He'll throw out all my stuff, not that there's much, but I have a couple pictures of Mom and Dad that I'd —" Cutting himself off, Horace took another sip of wine.

"You can't go alone, anyway," Donovan countered, rubbing up and down his mate's back soothingly. "Give me a day or so to regain my strength. Then I'll take you there to get anything you want."

With wide eyes, Horace peered up at him. "Really?"

"Absolutely," Donovan confirmed. If getting a few pictures would make Horace happy, then he would get it done.

"Thanks," Horace whispered, a small smile curving his lips. His shoulders sagged a little, and he seemed to relax against his chest again. "Oh." Straightening a little, Horace focused on Kontra again. "I have a shift at the grocery store tomorrow. I need to be there to start at nine." Glancing down at himself, Horace frowned. "I'll need to go home to get clothes before then."

When Horace nibbled his bottom lip, Donovan wanted to take his mate's mouth and do a little nibbling of his own. He felt his prick thickening in his shorts. Hoping the comforter hid his response, at least a little, Donovan tried to focus on the conversation at hand.

"There's a few guys here who are about your size, Horace," Kontra told him with a pat to his knee. "We'll find something appropriate for you. How long is your shift? We can plan to head over to your old place after that and pack up what you want."

"You'll really have me move in with you all, just like that?" Horace sounded completely shocked.

Kontra nodded. "Yes. Just like that." He pointed at Donovan. "Even if you don't bond this evening, you're still Donovan's mate. You will eventually. That makes you one of mine." His voice lowered to a growl. "And I protect my people . . . always." Then Kontra snorted, and a smirk curved his lips. "Besides, there are plenty of my guys who enjoy putting bigots and assholes in their place." Easing off the bed, Kontra patted Donovan on the knee. "Try not to worry too much,

Horace. You're not alone in dealing with Herbert and his friends anymore."

Once Kontra had left, Horace peered up at Donovan. He had a look of awe on his face even as his scent told Donovan that he was feeling a little overwhelmed. Donovan continued to pet his neck and back, hoping to soothe him.

"Wow, I—" Horace scoffed softly, sagging against Donovan. His next words came out so quietly that, if Donovan hadn't been a shifter, he didn't think he would have heard them. "I definitely didn't expect my day to turn out like this when I woke up this morning."

Donovan gave in to his need to explore Horace's flesh. Dipping his head, he pressed a light kiss to the side of his mate's neck. Moving his lips in a rhythmic nuzzle, Donovan suckled ever-so-lightly.

"Mmmm, you taste good," Donovan whispered, enjoying the flavor of man with a hint of salty sweat. "So good."

Horace shivered in his hold, his grip on Donovan's upper arm tightening and loosening spastically. "Oh," he whispered, a tremble working through his human for a new reason.

Recalling that Horace was a virgin, Donovan wondered if it was in every way. "Have you ever been kissed, Horace?"

"N-No."

Upon hearing Horace's murmured admission, Donovan groaned softly. "Oh, my mate."

The human that Donovan hoped to soon make his lover tensed in his hold, and he knew his mate had misunderstood.

"I look forward to teaching you everything, Horace," Donovan rumbled, nuzzling his cheek along his human's neck. "I can't tell you how excited it makes me" — his cock was practically throbbing behind the fly of his shorts — "that I will be the only one to ever have the joy of loving on your beautiful body."

"Y-You don't mind that, um" — Horace's breathing hitched for a second when Donovan nibbled his way up to the sensitive skin behind his ear — "that I d-don't know what to do?"

"I'll teach you everything, Horace," Donovan assured before suckling light on his earlobe. When his mate shuddered, moaned, and tipped his head to the side to offer more room, Donovan's heart sped up wildly. "We'll explore anything you wish together."

Horace moaned softly, another shudder hitting him. "Wh-What if I-I'm not e-enough?"

Realizing they had a smidge more to talk about, even though his dick didn't like that idea at all, Donovan lifted his lips from Horace's delectable flesh. He cradled his mate's jaw with his right hand and urged him to meet his gaze. The arousal swimming within Horace's hazel eyes was tempered ever-so-slightly by uncertainty.

Can't have that.

"The men downstairs," Donovan began slowly because he was having a hard time getting his thoughts in order with the amount of need and lust surging through his veins. "They explained what mates are to a shifter and that you are my mate? The other half of my soul?"

Horace nodded.

"Then it's as simple as that, Horace." Donovan threaded his fingers into Horace's dirty-blond hair, using the move to tug the band from his locks, freeing his strands. "I'm nearly two hundred years old, and I've been waiting for you for a very, *very* long time." Seeing Horace's hazel eyes widen a smidge, Donovan smiled at his human. "Yes, I've been around a while, and now that I've found you, I want to spend the rest of my centuries-long life using my knowledge to please you." He rested his forehead against Horace's and whispered, "Will you let me do that, my mate?"

To Donovan's pleasure, his mate said the sweetest words he could have ever heard.

"Yes, please."

With a groan, Donovan lifted his head only to tilt his face and seal his lips over Horace's, giving his mate his first-ever kiss . . . allowing him to taste heaven.

CHAPTER SEVEN

Horace's senses sang in bliss as he sank into Donovan's kiss. The big man teased his lips over his own, massaging lightly. Then he nipped lightly on his bottom one before suckling the flesh.

When Donovan nipped harder, Horace gasped. That seemed to be exactly what he wanted. He soon found his mouth filled with Donovan's tongue as he explored him. Donovan lapped at him, teasing his tongue, and his flavor exploded across Horace's tastebuds.

Unable to help himself, Horace moaned his pleasure. He pushed harder against the other man's mouth. Moving his tongue, he tried to match the man and do a little exploring of his own.

To Horace's pleasure, Donovan slowed the kiss and let him lead. Although he felt a little clumsy doing it, Horace dipped into Donovan's mouth. He licked along his teeth, then deeper, trying to explore everywhere.

When Donovan gently suckled on Horace's appendage, he moaned and shuddered. Tingles erupted, flowing down his arms and chest. His nipples beaded, and heat suffused his body.

Horace trembled once more . . . then felt something cold splash his hand. Jerking his lips away from Donovan's, he looked down. Heat suffused his cheeks for a different reason when he realized he'd spilled wine across his hand, having completely forgotten that he still held his nearly empty wine glass.

"Easy, sweetheart," Donovan crooned. "It's just fine."

Donovan carefully took the stemware from Horace's hand. With a wink, he brought it to his lips and finished the last swallow. He hummed and smiled as he set the glass onto the tray with all the other forgotten drinks. Then Donovan gripped Horace's wrist in a gentle hold and brought his hand to Donovan's lips.

Sticking out his tongue, Donovan slid the warm, wet appendage across Horace's hand, cleaning the remaining wine from his fingers. "There we go," he murmured, licking between Horace's fingers. "Clean again."

Goose bumps broke out on Horace's arms from Donovan's ministrations. His breath stuttered in his chest, and he almost felt a little light-headed. He felt his dick twitch behind his fly, and he whimpered.

"I love the noises you make, Horace," Donovan told him, a husky note in his voice. "Can't wait to hear what else you may make."

Then Donovan skimmed his hand down Horace's torso. His hand reached the hem of his shirt, pausing there. Holding Horace's gaze, Donovan slipped his fingers under the fabric and teased along his stomach.

"Oh," Horace gasped, his stomach muscles fluttering beyond his control at the feeling.

"Yeah." Donovan's deep gray eyes narrowed. "Noises just like that." Sliding his hand up a little, he skimmed his thumb along Horace's lower ribs. "Can I take your shirt off, Horace?"

Swallowing hard, Horace nodded.

"I need your words, my mate," Donovan told him, holding his gaze steadily. "I won't do anything without permission."

Horace had to swallow again before he managed to get enough moisture into his throat. "Yes, please."

Donovan growled softly, his smile turning feral. "Then

take off your flannel over-shirt, my mate," he urged as he began sliding his second hand under the back of his shirt.

For a second, Horace froze. Tingles skittered up his back upon feeling Donovan's light calluses scrape over his spine. Then he quickly shucked his flannel, dropping it on the comforter. Donovan made quick work of his shirt, placing it next to his flannel.

"Oh, Horace," Donovan crooned, his gaze running over him with obvious appreciation. "Look at all your lean, toned flesh." He didn't seem to need a response, which was good because Horace wouldn't have been able to give him one. Donovan skimmed the back of his fingertips over his chest, hitting a nipple in the process. When Horace sucked in a sharp breath, his bud tightening further, Donovan groaned. "Oh, Horace. Sensitive. So perfect."

"Will you straddle my lap, Horace?" Donovan asked, moving his hand to the edge of the comforter. "I wish to feel your flesh against mine."

Horace shivered in anticipation, more than on board with that. Easing sideways, he got to his knees. He groaned as the material of his jeans pressed painfully against his engorged shaft. Lowering a hand, Horace cupped himself through the stiff material, trying to adjust his erection to a better position.

"Gods, that's sexy," Donovan growled, his gray eyes having darkened to the color of storm clouds. Patting his lap, he ordered, "Come over here."

Glancing where Donovan indicated, Horace found his focus riveted to the bigger man's lap. The shifter had pushed down the comforter, revealing that he wore a pair of jogging shorts . . . and they were tented . . . obscenely . . . showcasing a very long, very thick shaft. As Horace stared, the huge, hidden pole flexed, moving the fabric enticingly.

Horace's ass clenched, and he couldn't even see the man's

true size. At the same time, he felt his fingers twitch in anticipation. He wanted to shove down the shorts and see the man's hard cock in all its glory.

"Gods, Horace," Donovan stated on a moan. "Love the way you're looking at me." Holding out his hand, palm up, he asked, "Will you straddle me?"

After licking his lower lip, Horace girded up his courage and took Donovan's hand. He swung his leg over the other man's thick thighs. Before he could settle, Donovan gripped his hips, making him pause.

Donovan dipped his thumbs into the waistband of Horace's jeans, teasing the flesh of his grooves. "Can I open your fly, Horace?" Donovan asked, his voice low and husky. "You'll be more comfortable."

Horace nodded quickly. Seeing Donovan's dark-gray eyebrow arch, he recalled the man's request for words. "Yes, please," he murmured. "Oh, god, yes."

Growling once more, Donovan didn't waste time. He quickly popped the button on Horace's jeans. In the next instant, he eased the zipper down. Immediately, Horace's erection caused them to separate, revealing his boxer-covered cock.

"Mmmmmm, I bet this is a thing of beauty," Donovan murmured appreciatively as he skimmed the back of his forefinger up the top half of Horace's cloth-covered shaft. "I can't wait to suck it as I finger your ass."

Once again, Horace felt his chute muscles clench. At the same time, his shaft twitched. He knew at least part of him wanted that, and wanted it badly.

"Come here, sweetheart," Donovan urged, moving his big hands back to his waist and easing him down and forward. "I want to feel you against me."

Upon the first press of Donovan's thick erection against his own smaller cock, Horace groaned loudly. His blood fired in his veins, and he shuddered as he squirted a dollop of pre-cum. His balls rolled and began to tighten.

Horace tried to breathe through it, to get himself under control. Except, then Donovan wrapped one arm around his waist and pulled him forward, flushing their torsos together. He tightened that arm, increasing the intense pressure against Horace's aching length.

Clenching his hands on Donovan's shoulders, Horace bowed his head. He pressed his forehead into the bigger man's collarbone. Whimpering, Horace fought the tingle already forming at the base of his spine.

"Don't fight it, Horace," Donovan murmured into his ear. "I'm right there with ya."

Then Donovan latched his mouth onto the sensitive skin behind Horace's ear, and that was all she wrote. His body went up in flames. Goose bumps broke out on his limbs. The hairs on his neck stood on end. Unable to help himself, Horace bucked his hips once, twice, and his orgasm rolled through him with such intensity that he cried out sharply.

"Oh, Horace," Donovan moaned into his ear. "Yessssss."

Even floating on the endorphins of the best release of his life, Horace still felt Donovan's big body jolt beneath him. The huge man growled and bucked up against him, then let out another low hiss. A second later, Horace felt teeth at his neck.

Horace had been warned that shifters claimed with a bite, but he still wasn't ready for it. Upon feeling the flash of pain, he cried out and froze. Then Horace felt Donovan's tongue lap around his embedded teeth, and the sweetest tingles flowed down from the area.

"H-Holy shit," Horace squeaked as his gut clenched. His balls heated and rolled, then tightened. A second orgasm blindsided him, and Horace called Donovan's name as he unloaded into his underwear once more.

Panting harshly, Horace rode out wave after wave of euphoria. He shivered in Donovan's hold, feeling as if every suck the shifter made to his neck transferred straight to his cock. As he floated, he absently wondered if that was what a blowjob felt like.

Recalling Donovan's comment about sucking him, Horace figured he would get to find out before too long.

Finally, Donovan eased his teeth from Horace's flesh. He shivered upon feeling the odd sensation, then trembled when the shifter lapped over the area. After several licks, Horace shivered for a new reason. The lapping over the area Donovan had bitten felt good—better than good.

Holy shit! It's turning me on again!

After a few more licks, Donovan stopped and let out a low, husky chuckle. "Wow," he mumbled as he nuzzled his cheek against Horace's neck. "So amazing, my mate."

"I-Is it a-always like that?"

Donovan threaded his fingers into Horace's hair. Gently, he used the hold to urge him to lift his head and meet his gaze. The warm smile and happy twinkle in Donovan's deep gray eyes eased Horace's embarrassment at unloading in his jeans . . . twice.

"It's always intense between mates, Horace," Donovan told him. He teased the fingertips of his other hand over the mark he must have left behind. "And this." Once again, a shiver of sensual awareness washed down Horace's chest, and Donovan told him, "This becomes an erogenous zone, but only when you or I touch it."

"Wow." Horace knew he'd been told a lot of information while eating dinner with the guys, but he couldn't remember if that was mentioned. "Th-That's a-amazing."

"It is." Meeting Horace's gaze, Donovan grinned at him. "Can't remember the last time I came in my clothes." He didn't look at all put-out. Instead, he continued to smile widely at him. "Probably for the best. I'm sorry to say, I don't have the energy or coordination to pleasure you like I want to for your first time."

Horace shivered upon thinking about what Donovan meant. "Um, okay."

Horace didn't mind the reprieve, either. While Horace wanted everything Donovan offered him by bonding with him, that was still a scary step to take with a guy he'd just met a few hours before. The guys downstairs had explained how Donovan had been captured and trapped, and how he'd be weak for a couple of days as he acclimated to his human body once more.

Easing back a little, Horace offered, "Why don't you just lie there while I clean us up."

Donovan groaned softly. "I want to care for you, my mate."

Taking the initiative, Horace pecked a kiss to the bigger man's lips. "You will soon enough. Me doing this while you're recovering doesn't change that." After another peck, Horace eased off the bigger man's lap and set about cleaning them up.

Secretly, Horace was ecstatic because that meant he could ogle Donovan's cock to his heart's content.

CHAPTER EIGHT

Donovan roused slowly. Horace's sweet scent filled his nostrils, even though he realized his arms were empty. His fingers twitched, and he reached across the bed. Finding it empty, Donovan snapped open his eyes.

Heat curled in Donovan's gut, and he fought against his urge to shift his legs restlessly. A second later, he felt it again. Something hot and wet moved up the side of his morning wood . . . which was no longer morning wood but hard as a steel pipe.

Snapping his attention to the comforter covering him from his chest down, Donovan spotted the obvious bump curving the blanket near his groin. He swallowed hard, feeling the tentative touches once more. Donovan groaned, realizing what was going on.

My mate is exploring my cock.

Oh, fuck. I gotta see this.

Slowly, so as not to surprise his inexperienced human, Donovan slid his hands under the comforter. He pushed down steadily . . . and down . . . until he revealed an absolutely gorgeous sight. Horace rested on one forearm while leaning over Donovan's groin. His lover skimmed his fingertips over his hard cock experimentally, touching and stroking far too lightly now that he was awake. Horace even still had his tongue out from when he'd licked him.

Horace paused, peering at Donovan from beneath his lashes. His smile appeared a little uncertain, but it was there. Donovan didn't leave him wondering if he liked what his mate was doing.

"Gods, sweetheart," Donovan rumbled. "I could wake up like this every morning and die a happy man."

A pretty blush darkened Horace's neck and cheeks even as he went back to his exploration.

It took every bit of self-control Donovan possessed to allow Horace to go at his speed. He desperately wanted to feel his mate's lips wrapped around his weeping knob. His cock ached for tighter stimulation than what Horace's light strokes offered. Donovan wanted to take control in the worst way, but he knew Horace needed to do this on his own, too.

Gotta let him build confidence.

Letting out soft groans, grunts, and growls, Donovan shared how wonderful he found Horace's touch. He shivered and shuddered, twitching on the sheet. His hisses filled the air with his other noises as his cock jerked and leaked from his mate's actions.

"G-Getting close, my mate," Donovan warned, his balls beginning to tingle with pleasure. Unable to help himself, he urged, "Tighten your grip just a little."

When Horace obeyed, Donovan let out a long groan. His balls pulled tight, and a hard shudder jolted him. He hissed Horace's name as his orgasm swelled through him, and he painted his stomach and chest with his release.

As Donovan floated with pleasure, he let out a soft sigh. Reaching down, he threaded his fingers through his mate's hair. He gently scratched at Horace's scalp, watching as his mate stared at his spilled seed, and he wondered what his human found so interesting about it.

A second later, Donovan found out.

Horace leaned forward, stuck out his tongue, and lapped at a glob of seed.

Donovan groaned as arousal surged anew upon watching the provocative sight. His mate cleaning him was the most erotic damn thing he'd ever seen. His stomach clenched and released, and he felt his dick swell once more.

Fierce need rushed through Donovan, and he racked his lust-fogged brain for how to move things along.

Lube first.

Reaching to the left, Donovan yanked open the nightstand drawer. He crunched up just enough to peer inside but not enough to disturb Horace with his task. Spotting the tube of lubricant, Donovan grabbed it with a growl of pleasure.

"Will you swing your ass up here and straddle my shoulders, Horace?" he asked, meeting his mate's gaze, hope filling him. "I want to suck you while you clean me." Holding up the lube, Donovan added, "And I want to open up your ass."

Horace stared up at him, his hazel eyes dilated, hunger swimming within them. Still, he hesitated.

For an instant, Donovan worried he'd pushed too hard.

Then, to his relief, Horace nodded. He started crawling up the bed, his movements a little tentative. Still, Horace followed Donovan's guidance as he gripped his hips and urged him to swing around.

Once Donovan had Horace where he wanted him—his knees on either side of his head with his long, pretty prick hanging in front of his face—he moaned as he popped the lid on the lube. He quickly poured some onto the fingers of his right hand. At the same time, he lifted his head a bit, stuck out his tongue, and lapped over his mate's damp crown.

Horace squeaked and jolted, obviously not ready for the move.

Donovan hummed, enjoying the light flavor of Horace's pre-cum. Resting his dry hand on his lover's hip, he held him steady. Then, with a little pressure, Donovan helped his mate bring his prick back to where he wanted it—close to his mouth.

As Donovan gently wrapped his lips around Horace's dick, he rubbed over his flank soothingly. He sucked lightly at first, testing his mate's sensitivity. Hearing his mate's moan, feeling the shudder that went through his human, Donovan hummed appreciatively.

Horace whimpered, his hips bucking.

Donovan took Horace's length easily, letting his mate do as he willed to his mouth. At the same time, he brought his lubed finger to his mate's opening. Using over a century and a half of experience, Donovan slipped his finger in and found his prostate on the first try.

Barking a cry, Horace jolted above him. He began fucking Donovan's face, his hips moving a little spastically, telling of his lack of control. Taking advantage of his mate being out of his mind with pleasure, Donovan slid a second finger in beside the first. He worked Horace's pleasure nub while stretching his mate, beating out the pain of the stretch with the bliss he created.

Far more swiftly than Donovan anticipated, he heard Horace cry out, the noise one of ecstasy. He tasted the salty cream of his mate's release as he filled his mouth. Swallowing, Donovan barely kept up with the thick bursts filling his mouth over and over.

Donovan eased a third finger into Horace's ass, using his orgasm to cover any discomfort he would feel from the stretch. All the while, he continued to tease and glance over his mate's prostate. He continued to suckle lightly on Horace's crown, tapping his frenulum and keeping him stimulated.

"Oh, god. Donovan!" Horace trembled above him. "I-I . . . I don't kn-know wh-what I n-need."

Popping off Horace's dick, Donovan rumbled, "I know what you need, my mate." He eased his fingers out of Horace's chute. "I'm gonna claim you now."

Feeling a whole lot stronger after a good meal and a fantastic night's sleep, Donovan easily manhandled his mate. He gripped Horace's hips and turned him around. At the same time, Donovan rolled to his knees.

Placing Horace on his stomach, Donovan levered over him and kissed the gorgeous claiming scar he'd left the evening before. "The first time is easiest in this position," he purred huskily into his mate's ear. "Is this okay?" Donovan moved into position behind him, allowing Horace to feel his hard shaft slide along the inside of his thighs.

Horace trembled in his hold, and the scent of his arousal perfumed the air. "Y-Yesssss," he hissed, arching his back. Then he whispered the admission, "H-Have wanted this f-for so long."

"You're mine, Horace," Donovan declared gruffly, fighting his urge to snarl at the thought of Horace wanting to couple with anyone else. He knew it was irrational. Still, as Donovan grabbed the lube and poured more onto his hand, he repeated, "All mine."

Donovan made short work of greasing up his shaft. Then he returned to Horace, pressing his chest to his back. He touched the crown of his cock to his mate's prepared hole.

"Tell me I can have you." Donovan came as close to begging as he'd ever come in his life. "Tell me I can slide my cock deep into your body and claim you."

He ached with need, his pre-cum flowing freely.

"Yesssss," Horace urged, rocking back toward him, putting pressure on Donovan's dick. "Want you. Make me yours, Donovan."

Horace's words were music to Donovan's ears. He didn't ask twice. Instead, he urged, "Push out, my mate." Then . . . he thrust.

Immediately, Horace's hot, silky channel opened to him. His wide head popped inside his mate. Growling his mate's name through gritted teeth, Donovan forced his body to still.

"Oh, god," Horace whined, concerning Donovan until he

heard him say, "Don't stop. God, please don't stop." To Donovan's surprise, Horace rocked back toward him again, taking another couple of inches. "Yesssss!"

Shocked and pleasantly surprised, Donovan thrust. He sank balls-deep into his mate's hot, tight body. When he bottomed out, he moaned. With one arm banded firmly around Horace's chest, Donovan held his human tight against him.

"Oh, god. Oh, god. Oh, god," Horace chanted. A shudder worked through his human. He whined and wriggled, rolling his hips a bit. "D-Don't stop," he pleaded. "So good. More."

"Fuck," Donovan hissed. "You're a fucking natural bottom."

"Yessss," Horace murmured, rolling his hips once more. "Feels so good when you move in me. So good. Want to feel more."

Donovan couldn't have been more shocked — or pleased — by this development. His mate didn't seem to have any pain, even from his first breach. Instead, fucking seemed to light up his nerve endings, leaving him begging for more.

Giving Horace what he wanted, Donovan eased partway out only to drive back into him. His mate moaned deeply, shuddering and shivering. Donovan did it over and over and over, his own ecstasy soaring as the heady scents of Horace's pleasure invaded every bit of his senses.

The milking squeeze swiftly went to Donovan's head. He could feel his orgasm threatening. His canines lengthened once more in preparation of biting his mate, resealing their bond. Donovan couldn't remember ever losing his control so swiftly and didn't know if it was due to being with his mate or due to his long-forced abstinence.

Doesn't matter.

Needing Horace to come first, Donovan reached beneath him. He gripped his mate's cock in a firm hold and began stroking him in time with his ruts. Donovan adjusted his angle until he nailed Horace's prostate with each thrust. Then he sucked on the claiming scar.

Horace shouted and tensed. His body bowed and bucked. He called Donovan's name, his cock thickening and jerking in his grip, his hot cum splashing over his fingers.

With his mate's pleasure perfuming the air, Donovan gave in to his own need. He thrust hard, embedding himself as deeply as possible. His balls pulled tight, and his cock throbbed. In harsh, gut-clenching bursts, Donovan coated Horace's rectum, marking his mate. Sinking his teeth back into his claiming scar, he reaffirmed their connection as he finished their bonding.

As Donovan took a couple of swallows of his mate's life-giving nectar, he moaned his bliss. His senses sang, and his elephant bugled triumphantly in his mind. His mate was there, in his arms, claimed and bonded, to be by his side for all time.

Donovan hummed as he eased his teeth from Horace's flesh. After resealing the bite mark, he nuzzled his mate's neck. He breathed deeply, reveling in their combined scents of arousal, seed, and masculine musk.

Absolutely perfect.

"Thank you, my mate," Donovan whispered into Horace's ear. Hearing his mate hum, he grinned. Carefully, Donovan eased them onto their sides, making certain his human wasn't in the wet spot. After kissing Horace's nape, Donovan quietly urged, "Just relax and catch your breath."

Horace clenched and released his chute muscles, pulling a grunt from Donovan.

"Y-You didn't pull out."

Grinning smugly, Donovan replied, "Nope. You feel too good." He pressed a wet kiss to Horace's nape once more before claiming, "Gonna lie here inside you for a while, then fuck you all over again."

To Donovan's pleasure, Horace moaned, "Yes, please."

Hell, yeah.

CHAPTER NINE

Horace knew he didn't look different, but he sure felt it. His ass twinged pleasantly with every move he made. That meant every time he scanned an item or bagged an item or bent with the scanner gun to run a large item still in someone's cart, Horace felt that wonderful twinge in his chute.

And I love it.

While it was proof that Horace had finally lost his virginity, it was more than that, too. His lover had been insatiable, and to be fair, Horace had been happy to make up for lost time, too. He had hickies on his chest and thighs, hidden under his clothes, and he knew he'd left a few marks of his own.

What wasn't all that hidden was Horace's claiming mark. The edge of the shirt he'd borrowed from one of the guys rested half on top of it. Horace felt damn grateful that it wasn't an erogenous zone if fabric touched it, or he would be at full salute all day behind his register.

As it was, Horace was tempted to touch it often. He appreciated the busy times when he didn't have the opportunity to think about it. Unfortunately, considering it was a Sunday, that didn't happen too often.

Out of the corner of his eye, Horace spotted movement as someone entered his lane. He straightened and turned toward the customer as she placed her basket on the conveyer belt. With the way she was looking at the magazine rack, Horace couldn't make out her face.

"Good morning, ma'am," Horace greeted by rote. He reached into her basket and began scanning items. "Did you find everything okay?"

When the woman turned to face him, Horace barely kept from cringing—Daphne. She was a regular at the backwater bar Herbert favored. He wouldn't consider her friends with his brother, but they definitely knew who each other were.

As if to reinforce that, Daphne narrowed her eyes at him. "Hey, Horace."

"Hi, Daphne," Horace greeted as he scanned the soft-shell taco shells. He racked his brain for something pleasant to say. "Are you enjoying the mild fall weather?"

Daphne smirked. "Yeah. I've still been wearing halter tops." With a wink, she leaned forward, waving her hand toward said halter top. "Shows my tits to perfection. Doncha think?"

"Uhhhh." Horace had no idea how to properly respond to that. He glanced at her chest. While he could assume her breasts were nice, they would never interest him. Finally, Horace stuttered, "Y-You look very n-nice."

Snickering, Daphne straightened. "Thanks." As she dug inside her purse for a way to pay, she asked, "So, is it true?"

Horace read off her total before asking, "Is what true?"

"Are you a fag?" Daphne inserted her card in the reader, then eyed him up and down. "That's what Herbert was ranting about last night." With a scoff, Daphne added, "I guess it would make sense. 'Cause now that I think about it, I never seen ya with a girl."

"I-I—"

Horace snapped his mouth shut. He felt his pulse spike. While he'd known that the memory Kontra had implanted in Herbert's mind had outed him, he certainly hadn't anticipated being faced with it at work. Horace's first impulse was to deny, deny, deny. Except, as he reached over and grabbed her receipt, he felt his ass twinge, and he knew he could never deny his lover.

"It's okay if you are." Daphne lowered her voice and leaned toward him. "Course, not everyone feels like I do, but I think those fags on that one TV show are great."

While Horace had no idea what TV show Daphne might be referring to, he found himself grateful for the weird sort of support. Taking a chance, he nodded. "Yeah. I'm gay." Keeping his voice just as quiet, he added, "And we don't like being called fags. It's, uh, well, if you're not gay, too, it's considered derogatory."

"Huh." Daphne took the receipt and shoved it into her purse. "I'll remember that." Then she picked up her bag of groceries and wiggled her fingers at him. "Toodles."

Horace lifted a hand. "Bye."

After Daphne had disappeared out the door, Horace turned back to his register and shook his head. "Okay. That was weird," he murmured. To his relief, another customer appeared, and he didn't have to think about it much anymore.

Time seemed to crawl by, slow and steady, and Horace found he kept glancing at the clock behind the manager's station. He had just over an hour left when the doors opened, drawing his attention. Feeling the blood drain from his face, he froze as he watched a red-faced Herbert stalk toward him.

Feeling trapped in his check-out stand, Horace could do nothing but stand there and wait. He could see the anger and disgust blazing out of his brother's brown eyes. His muscles clenched as he fought his instinct to flee.

"You a fuckin' cocksucker?" Herbert practically shouted the slur. He began rounding the end counter, obviously heading toward the opening of the cash-out stall. "My own fuckin' brother tryin' to parade around as a queer?" Herbert cracked his knuckles. "Not on my watch, ya ain't. I'm gonna—"

"Excuse me, Herbert." While Erin's voice was soft, tentative even, he did interrupt. "Horace is working right now." When Herbert pinned his angry gaze on Erin, the middle-aged man swallowed hard enough to cause his Adam's apple to bob. "I-I'm going to have to ask you to resolve family quarrels off of company property."

Herbert curled his lip at Erin. "You don't wanna get involved in this, Erin," he snarled, lifting a hand and pointing his finger at him. "My faggot brother needs to be taught a lesson."

"Well, that lesson can't happen here," Erin stated, his cheeks turning a dark shade of red as he glanced at Horace. "If you're going to buy something, please do so. Otherwise, I'm going to have to ask you to leave." After a second of hesitation, Erin added, "Or I'll have to call the cops."

Damn. Erin has more balls than I gave him credit for.

Growling, Herbert curled his lip into an ugly sneer. "Sheriff Johansson would agree with me." Except, he must have thought better of chancing it. Herbert leveled a hate-filled glare at Horace as he stated, "See you at home, brother."

A shiver crawled up Horace's spine as he watched Herbert stalk out of the market. His brother paused in the doorway, pinning a dark look on him. He lifted his hand and pointed at his eyes, then pointed back at Horace.

Once Herbert disappeared and the sliding doors closed, Horace staggered to the right and rested his hip against the counter. He inhaled and exhaled too swiftly. He focused on Donovan, recalling his lover's gentle kindness, and slowly managed to get his racing pulse under control.

"I'm gonna have to put a written warning in your file, Horace," Erin muttered, looking uncomfortable. "Bringing personal business into the store while at work and all."

Horace noticed that Erin wouldn't meet his gaze.

Whatever.

"I'm putting my two-week notice in today, anyway," Horace claimed. He'd written it up on paper borrowed from one of the guys. "It's not safe for me to stay here."

Erin glanced furtively at him, then looked away again.

"Good." As he walked away, Erin muttered, "Should have left before coming out. Moron."

Horace bit back a scoff. Erin didn't know how right he was. Except Horace hadn't come out. He'd been forced out by shifters that were just trying to be helpful.

Oops.

With a glance over his shoulder, Horace confirmed that Erin wasn't looking his way. He pulled out the burner phone Kontra had given him—since Herbert didn't allow him to keep enough money to buy a cell—and swiftly typed out a text. While Horace hated the scared rabbit sensation he was feeling, he knew he needed to give not only Donovan, but whoever Kontra intended to send with him, a heads-up about what they could be walking into.

A message came back almost immediately from Donovan.

Keep your head down, and don't leave the store alone. I'll be there as soon as I can.

Horace almost rolled his eyes.

Leave the store alone? Why the hell would I leave the store alone?

Still, he typed out that he understood and wouldn't be going anywhere.

Less than an hour later, almost as if it was in answer to his mental thought, Horace learned why he would leave the store.

The fire alarm went off.

Horace froze for several long seconds. It took him that long to even realize what the hell he was hearing. Then he had to rack his brain for his work's fire drill procedures.

"Snap out of it, Horace," Erin called, hurrying down another checkout lane. "Stand at the front doors and guide out anyone I send your way. I have to do a quick sweep."

"Uh, yes, sir," Horace replied on instinct.

Horace hurried toward the front sliding door and locked them closed. If he remembered correctly, he was supposed to let everyone out but not let anyone but the fire department in.

If I wasn't quitting, I'd think about brushing up on these procedures.

Seeing a woman with a child in tow hurrying toward the front, Horace quickly unlocked the door. He held it open for her. He was about to close it again when he saw a man hustling his way, so he put a hand on the door and waited.

A hand on Horace's arm yanked him out of the store. He stumbled, barely catching himself, before he spotted a big fist flying at his face. Pain exploded through his nose, and he bounced off the store's side. The back of his head smacked the wall, sending a second wave of pain through him.

Blinking and disoriented, Horace put a hand to his head.

"Told ya that would work."

Horace recognized the voice as one of Herbert's pals. An asshole named Ronan. He enjoyed pushing Horace around whenever he caught him alone.

"Good thinking," Herbert replied. "Pick him up. We need to get out of here."

In the distance, Horace could hear the sirens of the fire truck. The noise made his head hurt even more, and he moaned. When Ronan tossed Horace over his shoulder like a sack of potatoes, his stomach rolled, and he feared he would vomit all over the man.

As much as Horace thought it would serve the asshole right, he couldn't even guess at the beating that it would set in motion.

Horace managed to force back the sensation, but only barely. A few seconds later, he was tossed unceremoniously in the back of Ronan's *Bronco*. Then they were gone, climbing into the front.

With his head spinning, Horace wasn't able to make it to the door before the vehicle started moving. He bit back a whimper as the pain in his head intensified. As he lay there, trying to gather his strength, Horace realized something.

Herbert doesn't know I have a phone, so he didn't even check me for one.

Squinting through one eye, Horace made certain his brother and Ronan weren't looking his way. Then he carefully pulled out the device. He typed out a quick text to his lover.

Brother pulled the fire alarm. Kidnapped. Not sure where he and a friend are taking me.

Then Horace quickly silenced his phone, so any reply wouldn't alert his captors.

Keep your phone on. Kontra's guys will track you with it.

A second later, another message came through, filling Horace's heart with hope.

Keep your wits about you. I'm coming.

With that thought in mind, Horace glanced out the windows as much as possible, trying to figure out if he recognized anything. It was a little tough from his angle, but he thought they were taking him south out of town. When the vehicle turned and began bouncing down a rutted road, Horace knew he was in deep shit.

Horace kept his breathing slow and even, gathering as much strength as he could. As soon as the *Bronco* stopped, he shoved from the vehicle and sprinted into the swamp. He heard Herbert's shout, but he ignored it.

Hearing a gunshot, Horace hoped that Ronan's aim was as bad as Herbert's.

CHAPTER TEN

Donovan roared as he reread the message from Horace. Herbert had his sweet mate. He'd failed at protecting him.

"Calm down," Payson ordered, scowling at him from the front passenger seat. "We'll find him."

The hyena shifter was on the phone with Lamar. The peacock shifter was one of the gang's tech guys and was still at the house. According to Sam — the Texas longhorn beta — Lamar would be able to tell them exactly where to turn.

Lamar had a tracking device on the truck they were borrowing. It was owned by Olson, the man who also owned the Victorian they were fixing up. They used it when they needed to move building materials.

Evidently, Lamar also had the ability to track every single burner phone Kontra and his people utilized. The group had run into trouble many times over the decades. These days, they embraced technology and made it work for them.

"Take a right in two lights," Payson ordered. "We need to head south."

"Got it," Sam acknowledged. He glanced in the rearview mirror at Ryan, his mate. "Get ready."

Ryan dipped his chin in a nod. Then, to Donovan's surprise, the man opened the truck's rear slider window. The lithe male shimmied through, landing in the bed of the pickup.

"Turning right," Sam hollered.

In response, Ryan braced a hand on the window. Once

they'd turned, the dark-haired man focused his attention on a large case in the truck bed. He popped it open and began pulling out metal pieces. Ryan swiftly began putting them together.

Payson continued navigating for Sam. Sam would shout warnings to his mate. Ryan would brace as necessary while building . . .

Oh, holy fucking hell.

That had to be the biggest rifle Donovan had ever seen. "What is that?" he whispered, shocked.

"Ryan is ex-military," Sam stated, pride filling his voice. "He was a sniper. He ended up experimented on, making him an even better shot." With a cold chuckle, Sam glanced over his shoulder at his mate, who seemed to be checking his scope. "Even at these speeds on a rutted road, Ryan can hit what he's aiming at."

"A modified sniper," Donovan whispered in awe. He realized he still had plenty of things to learn about the people he was living with. "Wow."

Payson snickered as he ordered, "Left on this dirt road." Cocking his head, he mumbled, "Huh. You sure, Lamar?"

Donovan's shifter hearing allowed him to make out Lamar's haughty response. "Of course, I'm certain. Wherever Horace is, his phone is moving slower than a vehicle, but faster than the average walk. I'd say he's running."

"Then he escaped his—" Payson began but snapped his mouth shut a second later, only to growl.

Donovan had heard it, too. Someone was shooting. Feeling his elephant bugle in his mind, Donovan struggled to hold back his shift. He desperately wanted to give in, to allow his elephant to attack his mate's pursuers. Except, he was in a moving vehicle, and he didn't know where his mate or his human's attackers were.

"I have contact," Ryan declared, rising to place the rifle on the cab. He braced his legs and leaned forward. "Two males.

I recognize Herbert but not the other guy. Herbert is running into the swamp. *Other* guy is reluctantly following. Both are armed."

"Immobilize *Other* guy," Sam ordered. "Don't let him disappear into the swamp."

A second later, the report of a massive weapon left Donovan's ears ringing.

"Shit," Payson grumbled. "Forgot the fuckin' earplugs."

"Sorry," Ryan called. "He's down with a wound in the leg, but he's still holding a handgun."

"Can you shoot it out of his hand?" Sam asked as they turned one last corner, and an old, beat-up *Bronco* appeared before them.

Ryan snorted. "As if you have to ask."

Just as *Other* guy must have decided to shoot at them and bullets pinged into the metal of their pick-up, Ryan's huge rifle banged again. A pain-filled scream rent the air.

Donovan was out the door even before the truck stopped. The scent of his mate, coupled with the pungent odor of his fear, acted as a smack to his face. He didn't fight it. His shift washed through him swiftly, his clothes rending from his body as he expanded.

As soon as Donovan could focus, he swept his gaze around the small clearing that the assholes had parked in. He lifted his trunk and bugled loudly. Donovan paused and listened with his huge ears.

It was faint, but Donovan heard it.

Horace had called his name.

Ignoring Sam's shout, Donovan thundered in that direction. He noticed his mate's scent hung heavy in the air, the human's fear making it easy to follow. As Donovan thudded past the man Ryan shot, he heard his shout of shocked pain.

"Holy shit!" the man cried. "Did you guys see that? Did

you fucking see it?" He sounded unhinged. "It's a swamp elephant!"

"You're hallucinating due to pain," Ryan stated coldly before slamming the butt of his rifle against the human's head.

Donovan saw him slump to the ground before he was out of sight amidst the cypress trees. Moving swiftly, he shoved past trees and slogged through shallow water. His momentum kept him from getting sucked in by any of the mud, and he watched the telltale ripples of fleeing animals.

As Donovan pounded through the swamp, he noticed a hyena galloping alongside him. He ignored Payson in favor of focusing on his mate's scent. Donovan had heard that the hyena had the best nose out of the entire gang, so he figured the other shifter would keep him on track.

"Donovan! Run!" Horace appeared between the trees, jumping, running, and skidding around and over the twisting cypress trees. "Herbert has a gun!"

Donovan already knew that, but he loved the fact that his scared human's first instinct was to worry about him. As Horace neared him, Donovan noticed Herbert appear between the trees. The human paused, gaping.

Then Herbert's eyes narrowed, and a sneer twisted his features. "A fucking elephant," his sensitive shifter hearing allowed him to make out. "So much better than a wolf head."

Herbert lifted his weapon.

If Donovan had been in human form, he would have rolled his eyes. There was no fucking way the human's revolver would penetrate his hide. There was a reason that humans had invented something called an elephant gun.

His hide was damn thick.

Lowering his head, Donovan bugled as he charged. He thudded toward Horace, feeling the sting of a bullet hit his shoulder. Ignoring it, he continued.

Payson's hyena beat him to Herbert. The beast launched at

him, distracting him from shooting toward Donovan again. Somehow, Herbert managed to twist out of the way of Payson's attack. His mate's brother rolled twice before getting to his knees. The man pointed the weapon at Payson's pivoting form.

Donovan reached Herbert. Between one stride and the next, he swung his massive head. He slapped his thick trunk into Herbert's torso, sending the human flying through the swamp.

Herbert screamed. When he hit a tree trunk, the sound ceased. On his way down, Herbert hit a twisted cypress root jutting out of the water. The snap of bone echoed through the air. Then Herbert landed in the water with a splash.

The human didn't move.

Payson shifted and rose to his feet. Standing on the bank, the man scowled at Herbert's floating form for a few seconds. Then he frowned at Donovan and pointed at the human.

"You can go in there and get the asshole." Payson crossed his arms over his chest. "I ain't gettin' in there naked."

Donovan hesitated a second, then felt Horace's hand on his foreleg. Turning his attention to his human, he dismissed Herbert and Payson in favor of rubbing his trunk over Horace's body. He vocalized questioningly, hoping his mate understood what he needed to know.

"I'm fine," Horace assured, peering up at him. He rubbed over his leg, looking worried. "But you're bleeding." Horace swallowed hard as he eyed where a tiny bit of blood dribbled down his hide. "What can I do to help?"

"Eh. That ain't nothin,'" Payson claimed, stopping beside him. "Hold still. Looks like the bullet is just embedded in your skin here." Payson lifted his hand and hovered over the mark, meeting Donovan's gaze. "You ready for me to pop it out?"

Rumbling in acknowledgment, Donovan nodded his huge head.

Payson took him at his word. He dug a nail into the mark and popped out the small caliber bullet. Handing it to Horace, Payson ordered, "Put it in your pocket. We can't leave shifter blood out here."

"But what about?" Horace blinked. "Oh. It's already healed."

"Yep." Payson turned his attention back to where Herbert floated. "Now, will you get the asshole?"

Donovan rumbled irritably, but he took a step toward his mate's brother's body.

"Is he . . . dead?" Horace asked tentatively.

In the next instant, water churned. A few somethings grabbed onto Herbert's limbs, fighting over their prize. Donovan realized a trio of small alligators had found Herbert's bleeding form.

Within a few seconds, the water was still again, and Herbert was gone.

"Huh. Well, that solved that problem," Payson stated callously. He patted Horace on the shoulder. "Yep. Sorry, buddy. Your brother's dead."

"Oh, wow." Horace sighed deeply. "I don't know how to feel about that."

Donovan needed to comfort his mate, but his adrenaline still surged within him. He needed to stay in his elephant form. That way, he would be best able to defend him.

Instead of shifting, Donovan wrapped his trunk around Horace and tugged him close. He tucked him against his wide chest. Rumbling softly, Donovan used his trunk like an arm, petting and stroking him soothingly.

Horace petted him right back, running his palms over his hide. After several minutes of quiet, his mate sighed deeply.

"I know I'm supposed to be sad or something," Horace whispered, resting his temple against Donovan's chest. "I mean, he was my only family, but he stopped being a brother a long, long time ago."

"You'll grieve in your own way, man," Payson assured Horace, patting him on the shoulder. Maybe it was something in Horace's scent, seeing as he had such a well-developed sniffer, but Payson softly added, "And even if you don't, that don't make you a bad person."

Horace smiled faintly as he nodded. "Yeah. Okay." Lifting his chin, he peered into Donovan's eye. "Can we go home now?"

Donovan rumbled softly, loving that Horace considered the Victorian home . . . or maybe he meant being with Donovan was home. Either way, it didn't matter. Instead, he wanted to fulfill his mate's desire.

Lifting his foreleg, Donovan bent it in a step. Then he used his trunk to tap on it as well as his tusk. Finally, Donovan wrapped his trunk around Horace's waist and urged him close.

Horace must have figured it out. Reaching up, he grabbed Donovan's tusk. Stepping on his leg, he heaved himself onto it. He paused, perhaps considering, and Donovan used his trunk to point at his shoulder and the top of his ear.

After a few more seconds of guidance, Horace figured it out and clambered onto him, settling behind his head.

Happy to have his mate safe with him, Donovan strode back through the swamp. He internally smiled upon hearing Horace's laughter at Payson's hyena's antics as he bounced and romped beside them.

This is damn perfect. Me, my mate, and a walk through the forest . . . even if it is a cypress swamp.

After so many years, Donovan was happy, and he could smell that Horace was, too.

Yep. Damn perfect.

ABOUT THE AUTHOR

Charlie started writing fantasy when she was eight, and after stumbling onto her first erotic romance at age nineteen, she realized her true calling. She now focuses on writing gay erotic romance, normally of the paranormal variety, with heroes of all kinds. With the help and support of her husband, Charlie finally fulfilled one of her life-long goals . . . move to acreage with her horses. You can often find her curled up with her laptop and a cup of tea or glass of wine, creating her next adventure. Charlie enjoys exploring the mountains of her new Oregon home on horseback, 4-wheeler, or motorcycle.

She can be reached at ch.richards2010@yahoo.com

Or visit her at www.charlie-richards.com.